A TIME FOR GIVING

by Jill Briscoe

ACKNOWLEDGMENTS

Unless otherwise identified, all Scripture quotations are from the King James Version of the Bible.

Scripture quotes identified New American Standard are from the New American Standard Bible, Copyright © THE LOCKMAN FOUNDATION 1960, 1962, 1963, 1968, 1971, 1972, 1973, and are used by permission.

"Why Christmas" from PRIME RIB AND APPLE by Jill Briscoe. Copyright © 1976 by The Zondervan Corporation. Used by permission.

ISBN 0-89542-069-4 595

Copyright © MCMLXXIX by Jill Briscoe

Published by Ideals Publishing Corporation
11315 Watertown Plank Road
Milwaukee, Wisconsin 53226

Published Simultaneously in Canada
All Rights Reserved
Printed and Bound in the United States of America

Editorial Director, James Kuse
Managing Editor, Ralph Luedtke
Production Manager/Editor, Richard Lawson
Photographic Editor, Gerald Koser
Copy Editor, Sharon Style

Photograph on back cover by Russ Busby

Contents

"In the beginning was the Word, and the Word was with God, and the Word was God. The same was in the beginning with God. All things were made by Him; and without Him was not anything made that was made. In Him was life; and the life was the light of men. And the light shined in the darkness, but the darkness overcame it not. He came unto His own, but His own received Him not. But as many as received Him, to them He gave the power to become the sons of God" (John 1:1-12).

A Time for Giving

What are you giving for Christmas? God the Father scattered the Milky Way across the skies, hung Saturn's rings in place, and thought about Christmas. God the Son, working in unity with the Father in creative power fashioning the lumbering oxen and the gentle cow, thought often of the day that God would speak the Word, and He, "Christ," would be born. He would gaze with "baby eyes" upon the very creatures He had made. God the Holy Spirit, moving as a shadow upon the face of the waters in Genesis days, knew one day it would be necessary to move again. This time He would overshadow Mary's womb, that "the Holy thing" that should be born of her should be called the "Son of God."

All down the ages man was told about Christmas. He was told Christmas would be a time for giving. God would be giving Christ by the Holy Spirit, and men rejoiced. Adam walking with his God, oblivious to such names as Bethlehem, Herod, Egypt, Gethsemane, Calvary, chose in one appalling moment the company of Satan rather than the company of God, and the kingship of self rather than the Kingdom of God, and the bondage of sin rather than the glorious liberty of the children of God. It was there he heard his Maker's promise, "Christmas is coming, Adam." There in the garden he was told the promised Seed would bruise the serpent's head; and God the Father, God the Son, God the Holy Spirit, and Adam and Eve celebrated their very first Christmas.

Others of God's special people thought about God's gift and prepared their own personal presents. Not boxes decorated with tinsel, silver bells, and Father Christmases, but the welcome gifts of the promises of God about Jesus Christ. Jeremiah contemplated in quiet sadness the massacre of the infants, Hosea joyfully thanked God for the escape from Egypt, and Micah gave to the world the gift of the knowledge of the place of His birth. And think of Isaiah, He gave the gift of knowledge of the virgin birth and that He that was to be so miraculously conceived should be called rightly: "Wonderful, Counselor, the Mighty God, the Everlasting Father, the Prince of Peace."

Four hundred years later as Elisabeth was thinking about those promised gifts, God was busy wrapping up His Christmas present in Heaven in humanity's wrapping paper. He would be sending Him by very special delivery: God's gift. Christmas came early, just for Elisabeth. She had room in her inn for Mary, the outcast, ostracized, pregnant girl. God pulled the wrapping paper back just a little to let her have a peek at His present, and Elisabeth's baby leaped in her womb for joy, and she was filled with the Holy Ghost, with praise and with glory! And so she spake with a loud voice, "Blessed art thou among women, and blessed is the fruit of thy womb. And whence is this to me that the mother of my Lord should come to me. For, lo, as soon as the voice of thy salutation sounded in mine ears, the babe leaped in my womb for joy. And blessed are you for believing, Mary, for there shall be a performance of those things which were told you from the Lord" (Luke 1:42-45).

Encouraged and strengthened by her cousin, Mary, too, prepared. She believed the Anointed One must come, and soon, and by her holy character made ready to acknowledge her Messiah and yield Him her allegiance, as did other countless pious Marys of Israel. Because of her humility, she never in her wildest dreams imagined that she would actually become personally involved. But, you know, God couldn't have a Christmas without a Mary. He knew it wasn't enough to be devout, to attend the synagogue, to say her prayers, to know the facts. You see, He needed a body to live in!

> When God became a baby,
> He knew He'd to compress,
> His vastness, glory, all that power,
> Into littleness.
> A baby was the answer,
> But where to find one;
> The one who'd say, "be born in me;
> Oh, let me bear your Son?"

Would Mary be the earthly vehicle for His divine action? "Now, wait a minute," the devil must have whispered. "You've got everything going for you:

> You're engaged to be married,
> What will people say,
> When you say your baby
> Is conceived a new way.
> Just imagine their startled incredulity,
> When you say so sincerely,
> 'God gave it to me'!"

Mary bowed her head. She didn't heed. She bowed her will; she gave her body. She whispered, "Behold the handmaid of the Lord. Be it unto me according to thy Word."

Have you ever wondered how many Marys God watched and wondered about, and perhaps even asked, before He received His Christmas present of a body?

How many Marys, Lord, were there?
How many times did you try?
How often did Gabriel venture
Through the myriad stars of the sky?
How many miniscule humans?
How many a devout little maid
Heard your request for a body
And answered you thus so afraid.
"My love, Lord, you have it.
My will, Lord, 'tis thine.
I, to mighty Jehovah, my worship assign,
But my body, my body, my body,
  'tis mine."

How many Marys, Lord, were there,
Till Gabriel found her at prayer?
How many angels in glory,
Were wondrously envious of her?
And how did it feel, Lord, to see her,
And watch at your feet as she fell?
As she yielded her soul and her spirit
And gave you a body as well?
"My love, Lord, you have it.
My will, Lord, 'tis thine.
I, to mighty Jehovah, my worship assign.
And my body, my body, my body,
  'tis Thine!"

What are you giving for Christmas? God gave His Son, the prophets their promises, Elisabeth her praise, and Mary her body. What about Joseph? What did he give? Now, Joseph was thinking about Christmas. Oh, was he ever! Mary had told him about Christ, and the shock, the hurt, and the jealousy just completely engulfed him. How could he account for the confusing change in her character? This constant lying. These outlandish tales of angels, and lights, and God-given babies! How could he blame God for her sin? Tossing in torment upon his bed, Joseph decided to reject Mary and the baby. For religious reasons, of course! It just wasn't really respectable to accept Christ; but God knew His Joseph, his godliness, his honesty, his love for Him and for Mary. He knew he was a man who only had to be convinced of the truth by divine revelation; and then on the strength of a dream, he'd rise and give Christ his reputation and his

"I beseech you . . . that ye present your bodies a living sacrifice, holy, acceptable unto God . . ." (Rom. 12:1).

care for the rest of his life.

"But while he thought of these things, the angel of the Lord appeared to him in a dream saying, 'Joseph, thou son of David, don't be frightened to take unto thee Mary, thy wife. For that which is conceived in her is of the Holy Ghost. And she shall bring forth a son and you shall call Him Jesus, for He shall save His people from their sins'" (Matt. 1:20, 21). He did and, in return, received a personal knowledge and relationship with Jesus Christ, "Who being in the form of God thought it not robbery to be equal with God, but made Himself of no reputation, and took upon Him the form of a servant and was made in the likeness of men" (Phil. 2:6,7). This precious bundle of the "likeness of men" would require the gift of his protection and nurture. Joseph's first Christmas glowed brightly with reality and purpose, as perhaps ours did the day we, like Mary, received Him by His Spirit and, like Joseph, purposed to feed the new life within until Christ be fully formed in us. Joseph watched Divinity humanified.

How many Christmases passed? How many visits to the temple where Joseph first held Him in his arms and heard Simeon witness that his eyes had seen God's salvation? Maybe Joseph has something else to say to us, for he grew careless. Christmas followed Christmas, no more dreams, no more angels. Just the everyday routine of knowing Christ and living life until, twelve years later, he wasn't even conscious he'd lost touch. Two days' journey away, he suddenly realized his position and turned in true repentance, retracing his steps. What agony of heart, what longing for a sight of Him, a touch of Him, and when he found Him once again, oh, it was like that first wonderful Christmas once more. "Wist ye not that I must be about my Father's business, oh beloved earthly guardian of my life?" Oh, Joseph, you forgot! Why Christmas? You forgot my Father's business, your redemption. But now again, I will go home with you, submitting my life to your life in the exciting outworking of God's eternal purposes.

The party had begun! Herod was invited. "Bring your gifts," invited the wise men.

"Oh, I'd like to," said Herod, "but what should I give the King?"

"Your throne, your majesty. We left ours behind to fall on our knees, and acknowledge Him as King of our lives. Thrones make marvelous Christmas presents, especially when given with the gold of spiritual riches, and the holiness of frankincense, and the selflessness of myrrh."

"Find out the address. I'll be there with my throne," responded Herod.

And he came, but with his gift wrapped in hate and tied with murder. He came screaming, "I will not have this man to reign over me. I'll be my own ruler, in my own kingdom, and run my own life." And he gave his gift, the gift of rejection.

The shepherds gave their time. They ran in haste to give their time, to stumble down the hillside, in simple eagerness, to find out if all that heaven said about this earthly babe were true. Had God become a baby for them? Surely this was worth the gift of time. Time to leave their flocks, their daily work. Time to kneel before their infant Maker, to smell the smells in the dark cave, and realize He didn't care, He only loved so much He had to be born then. He couldn't wait for a "clean" white home at Nazareth. He knew how much obscure ordinary shepherds, like them, needed a gift for Christmas. "And when they'd seen it, they made known abroad the saying which was told them concerning the child, and all they that heard it wondered at those things that were told them by the shepherds" (Luke 2:20). The shepherds gave their time.

And the Innkeeper? This poor maligned man! He thought about Christmas. He did what he could. Mary and Joseph knocked on the door of his life, on behalf of Jesus Christ, one day, and they asked him to make room. And he did. He received Christ all right, and he gave Him a gift. What was it? His stable, of course. No question of giving the inn, that would have meant turning some people out. But he'd certainly like to have Him on his property, out in back with the garbage cans, where He wouldn't make too much noise and disturb his friends. "He ought to be jolly grateful to me," he thought. "He could be sleeping under the stars!" Even under the stars He made!

Christmas is for giving. God gave His son; the prophets gave their promises; Elisabeth, her praise; Mary, her body; Joseph, his reputation; Herod, his rejection; the kings, their thrones; the innkeeper, his stable; and the shepherds, their time. Tell, me, do you see your present there?

Room in my inn for my business affairs,
Room in my inn for my worries and cares,
Room in my inn for the drink and the smoke,
Room for the act, for the off-color joke,
Room for my family, room for my wife,
Room for my plans, Lord, no room for
    Your life,
And room for depression, when the party's
    all through,
Room for myself, Lord, but no room for You!
Room in my stable, Lord, room out of sight,
Room in the darkness and room where
    it's night,
Room with the cattle, the pigs, and the sheep,
Room where a newborn babe can't
    get to sleep;
Room with the dirt, Lord, the rats, and
    mice,
Room with the maggots and room
    with the lice,
Room, you can have it, how generous am I,
I like to be good when my Savior comes by;
Room in the filth and the mire of my sin,
Room on the Cross my redemption to win,
Room in my stable, but no room in my inn!

"*And an angel of the Lord appeared to him, standing to the right of the altar of incense. And Zacharias was troubled when he saw him, and fear gripped him. But the angel said to him, 'Do not be afraid, Zacharias, for your petition has been heard, and your wife Elisabeth will bear you a son, and you will give him the name John*" (Luke 1:11-13 New American Standard).

Room in My Time for Him

Did you ever doubt that the good news was good news? Zacharias did, and that is why he had nothing good to say about Christmas. He was literally struck dumb with doubt. That'll do it! Doubt and dumbness go together. Now Zacharias didn't for one moment doubt the good news wasn't good news at all. He knew it was sure to be good for someone. The nation of Israel needed to hear that their Messiah King was on His way and it was certainly good news to hear those rascal Romans would be getting their just desserts. It was just that he doubted the good news was good for him. Even when the angel identified himself as Gabriel, who stood in God's presence and had been sent specially from Jehovah with some good news for him and Elisabeth, he was "gripped" by fear instead of joy. In fact, after the angel had nearly frightened him out of his wits by appearing at the right side of the altar of incense, he had to calm the old man down by telling him not to be afraid. That was like saying "First the good news!" After all, it was good news to know there was nothing a sinful man needed to fear in the presence of such a holy being. But then it was as if the angel said, "And now the bad news!"—for he went on to tell Zacharias "Thy prayer is heard, and thy wife Elisabeth shall bear thee a son."

Now it wasn't bad news to know God had heard his prayer. He had to be glad about that! It was the timing of the answer he found trouble accepting as good news.

If he had been really honest, Zacharias would have said, "Oh God, your power and ability to answer prayer is not in question, but your timing is terrible!" In fact that is more or less what he did say, but the meaning is a little obscured by our King James English. "How shall I know this for certain? For I am an old man and my wife is advanced in years!" If we had been there, we could have asked him, "which years Zacharias?" and he would have had to answer "man years," for the problem with Zacharias was that he was thinking in terms of time rather than in terms of eternity. "Eternity time" is very different from "man time." Eternity's time is "proper time," the angel said so . . . . listen: "And behold Zacharias, you shall be silent and unable to speak until the day when these things take place because you did not believe my words which shall be fulfilled in their 'proper time'!"

God's clocks keep proper time—never fast, never slow, never stopping. We have to learn to live by that clock—by God's eternal calendar. We have to know that from human time to human time, God's heavenly alarm goes off and everlasting plans must supercede our human programming.

Man needed time to order his chaos aright

What is "man time" anyway? . . . God gave it,
    created it for us.
Dropped and suspended it in space, in the middle
    of eternity,
What makes it up anyhow?
    Ordered moments
      Packaged into minutes
        Growing to an hour
          Slotting into months of days
            Making tidy years go by.

and God gave it; but every now and then He has to remind us that He lives outside of it as does Christmas, God's hour, everlasting moment; time for the dawn to be born in the darkness of Palestine.

Zacharias, however, was struck dumb. Dumb with doubt. Doubt about his own personal involvement in the eternal purposes of Christmas and doubt about God's timetable.

Zacharias had lived a godly life a long, long time. He was thoroughly programmed into performing his religious duties; this was not to say that for him his priestly service was insincere. His religious disciplines were impeccable, and his devotion irreproachable. In the words of "timeless" Scripture: "They were both righteous in the sight of God, walking blamelessly in all the commandments and requirements of the Lord" (Luke 1:6 New American Standard).

But the problem was that he had almost programmed himself into permanence. He was in danger of being ruled by his own schedule. His holy habits had been so thoroughly practiced it was almost unnecessary for him to trust God anymore. At the end of a rigorous life of godly service, Zacharias could honestly have said it was easy to be holy and a joy to be obedient!

But to be programmed into permanent rituals is not the way to grow into new knowledge of God. Jehovah sometimes has to move in love on behalf of His very special children by introducing an eternal challenge into our easy management of time—pushing us out on risk's edge and forcing us to cling to Him. He wants us, however "old" a believer we may be, to reach for the impossible, away from the predictable possibilities that need no exercise of faith but simply a reaction of our own trained talents.

"So it was," the angel said to Zacharias, "This is your opportunity to put your faith in God in a way you have never had to before. He is offering you a part in His plan of redemption. Dare to believe, Zacharias, that He knows what He is doing, inviting you to be involved."

Now that sort of thing is bound to disturb a man's routine. Have you noticed how we are such creatures of habit? That is why we get so unsettled and insecure as soon as God chooses such wild times to do "His things" in our lives, to order a situation or relationship that will cast us upon God's resources. Think about Christmas for a moment.

It may have been God's "proper time;" but as far as man was concerned, it was inconsiderate, inconvenient, and inappropriate! In fact—a very "improper" time! That doesn't necessarily mean God's judgment was impaired! It just meant that the view from the limited dimension of earth did not give the people concerned a heavenly perspective.

If the dating of Christmas Day had been left to the participants in the event, the shepherds would no doubt have chosen to be off duty, the wise men would probably have wished they had been attending an astrology convention in Baghdad, and Mary would have requested that she be married. I even believe the kindhearted innkeeper would not have wanted the Romans to be having a census so that he would have room in the inn, whereas Anna the prophetess would long to be years younger so she could speak of Him to all who were outside Jerusalem as well as those within the Holy City. No, from man's perspective, it was certainly not the "proper time." But being the handmaiden or slave of Jehovah meant His time was to be their time; His plans and purposes, their plans and purposes; even their personal relationships and all their hopes and dreams must be subject to alteration or cancellation where heavenly appointments were concerned. When "disappointments" are "His appointments," we can accept God's intervention as normal and make room in our time for Him.

Our problem is we have no room in our time! It is full of other things. It was in the fullness of time God sent forth His Son; and for those whose time was full of God, it was a simple matter to rejoice. When the people involved had had time to look back upon that first Christmas and think about it, they would surely have rejoiced in the proper time that Jesus had arrived.

Religiously speaking, it was the proper time. Many in Israel had fallen away from the Father's faith. Zacharias knew the godly descendants of Jacob would welcome a preacher who could turn many of the children of Israel to the Lord again in preparation for the King's coming. John, his promised child, would be privileged to do this.

Politically speaking it was the proper time. It was past time to be delivered from the hated Roman yoke. A Savior was desperately being searched for by Israel who would "guide their feet into the way of peace."

Culturally speaking, it was the proper time. Roman roads made travel so much easier, opening up areas of the world that had hitherto been quite inaccessible. What is more, Rome offered her protection to travelers on these roads. The good news of Christ's coming could be quickly and safely spread to the four corners of the Empire, the Greek language helping to cut across communication barriers as new disciples gossiped out the gospel.

Socially it was the proper time. There were many family and national problems in Israel. "The hearts of the Fathers" needed to be turned back to the children and "the disobedient to the attitude of the righteous." People were looking for answers in their relationships at home and in their nation.

Personally it was the proper time. Upon reflection, the shepherds would be glad the angels came that night. They had time to listen, to leave their flocks at rest and "go and see this thing which had happened." The wise men would realize that they had learned to follow in simple faith, to be guided step-by-step and taught to seek and seek that they might find! Would such useful discipline have come to them if they had actually been on the spot? Had Mary been older she may not have so readily accepted the unbelievable challenge of a divine Baby, virgin born, and Anna's words would possibly have had little effect without the wisdom and respect her great age and consistent testimony afforded her.

Perhaps it was not such a bad time after all! But then they needed the faith to believe that. Proper time is never bad. How can it be when He who rules it, plans it out in love, and sends it ticking into the happenings of our lives?

As for Zacharias and Elisabeth, how good of God to wait until they were old and well advanced in years. They were so old they would be sure to be spared the news of their beloved son's head on a dish at Herod's dinner party. Yes, it is best that we know that God knows best!

Zacharias, who had been struck dumb with doubt, was, however, to know the freedom of

faith. For after a time he believed it was God's proper time after all! He wrote, "His name is John," thus accepting his involvement in eternal matters and "was filled with the Holy Ghost and with joy!"

This Christmas many of you are struck dumb with doubt. Doubt about the Good News of Christmas. Maybe you think it good for some-

one but you doubt it is good for you. Perhaps you think you are too old, too young, too bad, too good, too set in your ways, or too busy; then you need to make room in your time for Him. Maybe you cannot understand why God has allowed this or that to intrude into your tidy schemes or dreams. It all seems such awfully bad timing; but you see, you could yield your time to Him and then be able to say as David, "My times are in Thy hands."

I did that—put my time in His hands—hundreds of years ago when I was eighteen years of age! Christ was born in the cold cave of my heart. He brought light and warmth and a sense of time into the empty granite immobility that was my life. That sense of "going somewhere," of starting to "keep time" with eternity began then.

It began in between the white sheets of a hospital bed. It hadn't seemed the proper time at all for me to be sick. Studying at Cambridge, I was trying to get assignments finished and cram for the exam that faced me. How inconvenient, inappropriate, and inconsiderate of that pain to come then, ushering me into the emergency room where I was to be neatly packaged for healing and laid to rest in a big white ward. The cardboard-stiff clad nurses scuttled up and down polished wood corridors, looking like white bowling balls in a disinfected skittle alley. It was all so strange and not a little frightening. I was eighteen, too young to be seriously ill—at Cambridge, too far from home to be in a hospital—in the middle of important study, too busy to be missing classes—and yet, and yet, the alarm had gone off in heaven and the dawn visited me. "She that had sat in darkness saw a great light." Upon me, upon me did the light shine, and eternity took over at the *proper time!*.

Proper because I was only eighteen and had the whole of my life ahead to serve Him. Proper because even though I was far from home, that very fact forced me to cast my care upon a Heavenly Father and not an earthly one. Proper because that pain, allowed just then, extracted me from the busyness of a barren life, and gave me time to reflect on the claims of Christ.

Since my first real Christmas all those years ago, people have visited the "cave" of my life to see Jesus, or to share what they have learned of Him. The "shepherds" came, uncouth, roughly dressed teenagers with leather jackets and long hair and fierce strong faces. They came at the "proper time" instigated by God to investigate the possibility of "peace on earth"—of peace in particular on their earth. But when they came, I reacted like Zacharias. It may well have been the proper time for them to see the Peace-Child, but I doubted it was the proper time for me to show Him to them. I was a young mother with three children under the age of six to care for, with a husband whose business took him away nine months out of the year; but God showed me how to make room in my time for His business, and His gorgeous teenage shepherds who had simply come to the cave that they might worship the King. They came and I received them. They found the Christ and "went to make known, the statements which had been told them about this Child!"

The kings came to my cave to see Jesus, too. Important people, pretty ladies, svelt-suited gentlemen, rich beyond measure, wise after the wisdom of this world, yet led by a star that pushed and edged them on until they came to the place where the young child lay—the straw of my life. It was the proper time for them as well. Riches had brought only glittering fancies. Astrology had left them with larger questions than they began with; many had journeyed so far through life they could hardly bear the search anymore. It was time, proper time for the star to stop and for them to worship Him. But I must confess, on my part I doubted if it were the proper time for me. I felt inadequate, unsure of my abilities. My homespun garments couldn't match the splendor of their garb; their wisdom learned in strange exotic schools defied my simple mind. Yet God knew best, of course.

I would be no threat, no competition, no cause of envy or covetousness. There would be naught to distract their eyes from His beauty. And for me? My faith would grow, my faith in His abilities, not mine, to answer the wise, to show them the Christ and to open my mouth when brought before kings and have Him tell me *at that proper time* what I should say!

I think of other proper times. The time my sick mother-in-law needed to be cared for in a period of my life that could only be described as hectic man time! And then there was the child in deep distress that appeared at my kitchen door as I bathed my baby and watched two toddlers toddling into interminable trouble. I think of the homeless relative who needed a place to live and be encouraged, the group of ladies needing inspiration, the young married couple looking for help with a flagging marriage. I think back and I remember how, when I live my life according to God's clock, not mine, there must always be time for people; and when there is, the lessons that I learn, the blessing and the growth in faith will be my grand reward. But most of all, there comes to my heart at times like these, a quiet sense of precious eternal moments lent to me—here and now. God's great gift to me—the gift of "proper time"—is worth receiving.

They . . . "went to make known, the statements which had been told them about this child!"

"Now the birth of Jesus Christ was as follows. When His mother Mary had been betrothed to Joseph, before they came together she was found to be with child by the Holy Spirit. And Joseph her husband, being a righteous man, and not wanting to disgrace her, desired to put her away secretly" (Matt. 1:18-19 New American Standard).

Immanuel

Joseph was secretly thinking divorce—at Christmas! That's what the Bible says. How can this be, when many of our Christmas cards depict Joseph standing in manly grandeur, lovingly guarding his wife and the Christ Child? Well now, if we back up a little, we can see Joseph in a very different light. We can watch him sleeplessly tossing to and fro upon his bed, as he "considers this thing." What "thing" was he considering that chased his sleep away? Divorce. That will do it! I know nothing better designed to keep your eyes wide open when they should be closed, as that one dread word—divorce.

Joseph was betrothed to Mary. Betrothal for the ancient Hebrews was of a more formal and far more binding nature than the engagement is with us. In fact, among the Jews the betrothal was so far regarded as binding that if a marriage should not take place through some breach of contract, the girl could not marry another man until she had a paper of divorce.

So why, oh why, was Joseph thinking secretly of putting his wife away? What dreadful thing had come to threaten the relationship between himself and Mary? Quite simply put, it had been discovered that Mary was pregnant. The Bible says, she was "found to be with child by the Holy Ghost." It is obvious from the text, however, that by the time the news reached Joseph, the "by the Holy Ghost" bit was either not reported or, apparently, believed! One can hardly blame him either. No wonder he was secretely thinking divorce!

Notice he was "secretly" thinking. Actually the Bible says he desired to put Mary away secretly. It follows, though, that if he were thinking of putting her away secretly he was also alone in his ponderings. How lonely he must have felt—and at Christmas. Here he was still legally "attached" to a woman and yet planning, alone in his mind, how he could end his marriage. There can be no lonelier place than to be internally isolated with that sort of decision to make. Nobody knew how bad the situation was except the people intimately concerned. How could they know? Everything had been done decently and in order. The dowry had been paid to Mary's parents in a public ceremony. We don't know what the dowry was. It could have taken the form of service as, for example, Jacob's seven years of hard labor for his beloved Rachel in the Genesis story. Whether it had been so, or paid in goods, we know not, but we know it had been paid—for this was the central feature of the betrothal ceremony. There had been an acceptance before witnesses of the terms of the marriage contract. Publicly each had been committed to the other and the family knew, the village knew, Joseph's whole world knew they were married already. Now all that had to take place was the final wedding ceremony.

But what the whole world didn't know was that Mary had apparently been unfaithful to him. That heavy knowledge was Joseph's alone to bear toward his sad conclusion.

Let me ask you a question. Are you desiring secretly to "put away" your partner this Christmastime? Are you, like Joseph, silently considering divorce? Perhaps everyone around you thinks your marriage is in great shape, but you are saying desperately to yourself, "If only they knew" and then you are adding hastily to that last drastic thought—"if only you could stop them knowing!"

Maybe up to now everything has been done decently and in order in your relationship. The ceremonies and public witness are a thing of the past. Your whole world knows you are well and truly married; and, as far as they are concerned, all is well. How could anyone guess at the awful secret you have been locked up with, in the vaults of your soul?

It is usually the things we find out about each other—after the vows have been vowed and the music and dancing is through, and what the world outside knows nothing about that leads us to think of divorce!

It's like an old Cumbrian farmer from the hills of northern England said at a wedding I once attended, "You never know what you've got until you get them home and the door shut!" It's the things you learn of each other in the growing knowingness of holy matrimony that can lead one to consider the thing and, having considered it, desire to put him or her away secretly!

The first mistake I see Joseph making here was to retreat to "consider the thing alone." When traumatic events occur in a marriage relationship, the worst thing you can do is cut the communication lines with your partner. To be alone in awful isolation to consider your terrible dilemma, will not give you a balanced view of the situation.

It is obvious it did not give Joseph a true picture at all. What is more, the Bible tells us his decision to "put her away" was made at night and probably in a state of great emotional agitation—always a bad time to decide anything of importance. If only he could have given Mary time to

explain; but in this case, the solution to the problem was being sought for by "one" member of that union. There was apparently no adequate understanding of the other's explanations, however strange and wild they sounded! Now there is no doubt about it, it couldn't have been a very easy thing for Mary to share with Joseph. Just how do you explain the wonder of a normal human life beginning to manifest itself within one's body, never mind the miracle of the Incarnation! But sometimes when one just doesn't understand the other's viewpoint, you have to trust her integrity. Once trust flies out the window of a marriage, divorce is at the door. Joseph had disbelieved Mary. He had flatly refused her explanation of the hows and why of the situation of her pregnancy, even though he must have known her godly character well enough to know she would never lie to him. At this moment of crisis, he could not believe the best about her; and though I am sure he forgave her, he obviously refused to continue to discuss the matter.

When a point of conflict arises in a marriage, it is a very dangerous and destructive thing to terminate open and honest dialogue. Somehow you must keep talking. Mary and Joseph had not had very long to practice good communication, but I know couples who have lived together for years and years and years and still have a level of communication that never goes deeper than the weather or the price of the Sunday roast! If a young couple can only give time to talk before marriage and then continue to reveal themselves to each other with words after the ceremony of holy wedlock, then understanding and trust can grow. Words unveil our real being, telling the other person all about ourselves. Words tell the loved one *what* we are as well as *who* we are! For a word is a thought in the concrete, and a thought comes from within a man's reality. "What a man thinketh in himself—he is," says the Word. So it follows, if a man says what he thinks, the listener can come to know what a man is!

Joseph surely knew Mary's words sprang from a pure and truthful character. He had been used to her telling him the truth; yet in this instance, he did not accept her words as valid. At that time of conflict, what he knew of his partner should have been determined by the level of communication and the habit of truthfulness that had been practiced between them. Then he would have made a better judgment.

Maybe in your partnership there has never been any great depth of communication, and a bad habit of being deceitful has been formed. Then your marriage will really need help; and you will have to make a decision to begin to learn to talk now, before the final crisis comes. Try talking about things that *don't* matter; then when it is absolutely necessary, you might be able to discuss things that *do* matter. Some of you may have been saying to yourself, "It's too late; no one knows what it's been like shut up in this marriage with no one to talk to." But you *do* have someone to talk to! You have your wife or your husband—go on, start and talk about something! Anything as long as you start. But "how do you start" you may ask? A good way to begin is to ask a question.

If only Joseph could have asked a question, about anything. If only he had said, "What did the angel look like?" Or, "What was your reaction to the message you said you heard?" Then Mary could have expounded, filling in all the details of the picture, describing her terrible fear of this heavenly visitor or perhaps her troubled queries as to *how* this strange thing would be executed. Her lovely response could have been shared— "Behold, the handmaid of the Lord. Be it unto me according to Thy word"—adding credence to her story, for Joseph would be well aware of her sweet submissive spirit to Jehovah. I cannot believe that if Joseph had but given Mary a chance with words, he would have believed.

Joseph, however, was a man of "stern principle," a just man, a strict, obedient Jew. Facts were facts. He didn't give Mary a chance to explain; faith was faith and sometimes required of us mortal beings in the face of facts! He simply went ahead on his own and planned the divorce. Justice without mercy is often the "outraged" partner's response to what he believes is adultery. Especially if the man is a man of stern principle! Joseph was such. Let me hasten to add, Joseph, being an honorable man, was only thinking of Mary; for the Bible tells us clearly he was not willing to disgrace her publicly. Divorce appeared to be the decent and right thing for everyone's sake; and the Bible says, "after he had planned this, he fell asleep." The decision had been made and a certain unhappy relief permitted him a momentary respite of uneasy slumber.

Joseph, however, had a dream. It was the strangest thing that had ever happened to him. Men of stern principles don't usually go around risking their reputations on the strength of a dream! Many men profess not to even dream at all! I'm married to one of them! "I go to sleep to sleep, not to dream," my manly man says pragmatically, and appears to do so. But men of stern principles who tend to look at life sensibly sometime admit that the organized principles that rule their lives are occasionally interrupted by the "Principle Maker," and the craziest things can happen to upset the usual order of events and make a believer out of them. If Joseph had been asked about the rules of his life, he would have said that he lived a right life according to the law. He lived not by expecting visions and lights and angel's visitations, but by down-to-earth common

sense, seeking to obey the Ten Commandments and do unto others as he would them do unto him. It would not, I am sure, have been said of Joseph that he didn't believe in angels and lights and such things; he just didn't believe God would use that sort of media to speak to him—or to Mary!

But God did speak to him just like that! He came to Joseph in a dream, using an angel agent, and gave him a message about his marriage. Joseph learned you are never too old for a "first-time" experience where God is concerned.

First of all, he was told by his heavenly visitor not to hesitate to take Mary as his wife. "Joseph, son of David, " he was instructed, "do not be afraid to take Mary as your wife; for that which has been conceived in her is of the Holy Spirit." Accept her as she is, he was told, not as you would like her to be, or as you had dreamed she could be, but just as she is! Take her to yourself as you find her at this very moment, pregnant, upset, worried, hurt, and dismayed that you didn't understand or believe her. You need to establish one irrevocable fact in your head Joseph—Mary is *your* wife—no one else's, and you alone are responsible for her, for she belongs to you. Maybe you, too, need to remember your marriage vows: "to have and to hold, from this day forward, for better, for worse, for richer, for poorer, in sickness and in health, to love and to cherish, till death you do part."

Perhaps the words *worse, poorer, sickness* need to jump up in your memory and remind you of the fact of your commitment and duty toward the partner you freely chose as your own. To accept one's other half as you find him or her *after* the honeymoon is over is simply to be carrying through on the commitment made before the honeymoon began.

This can help start the healing of a broken marriage! "The honeymoon is over, now the marriage can begin," someone once said to a troubled young couple seeking help. All too often these days we hear "the honeymoon is over, now the marriage can end!" We start to understand each other as we begin to unveil ourselves with words, and believe and trust the truth of the words in the other. Then must come the acceptance of the one who is revealed as he is, however much of a shock that revelation is. The angel reiterated the shocking fact of Mary's pregnancy to Joseph, "That which has been conceived in her is of the Holy Ghost." "This is how she is Joseph," he said and "this is how God wants you to accept her. God is working in her life, for she is God's child; and you have the privilege of nurturing and caring for her as He works out His purposes in her." We have to start where we are with each other and go on and grow on from there.

Maybe you are saying, but my wife is no Mary; she did cheat on me. The principle is the same. She is still *your wife*, whatever she has done right or wrong, and God would seek to take you back in your dreams and your imaginings to your wedding day and the vows of commitment you made to each other. You must accept her as she is—*that* principle is the same—just as she has to accept you as *you are*, not as she hoped or dreamed or expected you to be.

Now God knows how hard this is going to be. How can I say that with such confidence? I can say it because I read the angel's words to a man who was wondering how on earth he could go through with such a thing. God knows how hard obedience is, but He knows equally well how to empower the act of submission to the command. "How then," you ask? God matches your two words with one: "Immanuel!" The angel told Joseph that Immanuel would come to his marriage. Immanuel means "God with us" and that is what it was going to take for Joseph to accept his wife as she was. Without God you, too, will probably go ahead with your secret plans of divorce; but "Immanuel" can make the difference just as He did that Christmas long ago. He can enable you to save your marriage. He will light up your understanding of each other as He is born into your home, uniting you in the common cause of caring for His well-being. Immanuel will trust Himself to you if you will trust yourself to Him in an eternal exchange of your lives.

The Bible says that Joseph awoke! He certainly awakened to more than the morning light. He awoke to the possibilities of a healed relationship with Mary and a marriage partnership with God as the chief Partner. He woke to the excitement of Immanuel making the difference, becoming the focal point of their days on earth and their final home in heaven. He woke to the commands of God and "did what the angel of the Lord commanded him, taking Mary as his wife. He kept her a virgin until she gave birth to a Son and then he called His name Jesus." Why Jesus? Jesus, because Jesus means Savior; "Jesus, for He shall save His people from their sins," the angel said.

Do you have a problem in your marriage relationship this Christmas? Do you toss to and fro upon your bed and plan your escape? Have your principles been outraged or has your heart been broken? Have your engagement plans crumbled around your ears?

Listen to the angel. Jesus is the Savior who can be born into your relationships. He can save people, any people from their sins. Sins of selfishness and pettiness and silly stupidnesses that wreck love. Sins of immorality or cheating or perversion that can smear the soul and body. Sins of coldness, hardness, and indifference that freeze friendship into immobility.

So you, too, have the option that Joseph had. Do not be afraid to take your partner to yourself, to reach out and put your arms around an estranged loved one, to remember he or she is yours. Then Immanuel will help you, by His power, to accept your partner as your marriage has revealed him or her to be.

If you can do that, you have laid the basis of a good partnership; and you will be ready to face a hostile world together. We are told Joseph and Mary did have their final marriage ceremony. "And Joseph arose from sleep and did as the angel of the Lord commanded him;" but we are also told their lives together were dogged with trials and troubles, for Herod sought the Christ Child's life.

Now we can be sure Herod always will. There will be many kings of the world that will seek to exterminate the life of God from a marriage. There will be the Herod of extra-marital sex, the Herod of boredom, or the Herod of indifference and misunderstanding. There will be the king of greed and lust, or the king of childishness or drink. In the words of Scripture, we can know "Herod is going to search for the Child to destroy Him."

Once a marriage is yielded to Christ and His principles, Herod is out to finish it. We, like

Joseph, will need to shield our family from him that would destroy us. Once Immanuel has become the light of our home and the meaning for our existence, we will know the hot pursuit of Herod. Joseph had to move his family out of the reach of that cruel monarch and flee all the way to Egypt. From there he had to keep a careful vigil for his enemy's approach, knowing his family's very lives were at stake. He listened and obeyed God's word, which helped him make all the decisions that needed to be made.

Maybe you are tempted to flirt a little at a Christmas party. Or perhaps you have taken a friendship a few steps over that permissible line that hems you into your own marriage. Herod seeks the young Child's life. His words may be as smooth as honey, as Herod's were to the wise men—but destruction was in his heart! You might have to remove yourself physically from temptation. That may mean saying no. No to the party or the social engagement where he or she will be. Perhaps there will need to be a job change. You may cause distress to a few friends, but better distress than disaster. God's Word will help you to make the decisions that need to be made. "Flee youthful lusts" the Bible says; then flee into Egypt if necessary. You may think that your marriage would never be attacked in this way. Surely once you decide to start having a marriage instead of a divorce, you think God would be so pleased He would protect you from all ensuing problems. But God tells us we can expect Herod; however, He also tells us to expect Him to be actively working for us in the middle of the problems Herod brings!

Behind Herod stands Satan, the great hater of the Christ Child and all He stands for. Christ is *for* marriage. It is His good idea. If Satan is against all that Christ is for, it follows he is intent on destroying marriage.

Then what can we do? You may say, "Our marriage is so fragile it will hardly stand the strain from within, never mind an onslaught from without." Remember Immanuel can be within. He will bind your hearts together as you unite to face the foe. The Book of Ecclesiastes puts it thus: "Two are better than one because they have a good return for their labor for if either of them falls, the one will lift up his companion, but woe to the one who falls and

when there is not another to lift him up. Furthermore if two lie down together they keep warm, but how can one be warm alone? And if one can overpower him, who is alone—two can resist him. *A cord of three strands is not quickly torn apart"* (Eccles. 4:9-12).

Together Mary and Joseph faced flight, murder, and exile in a strange land. They came through triumphant because God was with them. Two are better than one, but three are even better than two! He didn't save His own earthly family from trials and terror and neither will He save us from such; for Herod is alive and will be after us while we are a part of this groaning creation, awaiting our redemption. "Immanuel," carried and cared for in Joseph's and Mary's arms, brought the inner comfort, joy, and meaning for their existence as they faced the foe together. The young couple became one in purpose, for even though the Scriptures tell us two are better than one, they also tell us a mystery. Two *are* one when God joins such together in Christian wedlock. Those of us privileged to be married at this Christmastime can know we are really two halves of a whole—bound together by the Christ Child—*Immanuel.*

27

"The fear of the Lord is the beginning of wisdom: and the knowledge of the holy is understanding" (Prov. 10:10).

How Wise Is Wise?

The Wise Men were very wise—they were seeking Jesus. We think so anyway, for we believe in Christ. Other people, however, would consider them stupid, unintelligent, and superstitious. So what is a wise man? And just who is to decide how wise is wise? If we live our lives by speculation, we can come up with a thousand different answers to that question. If, however, we live our lives according to revelation, there is only one answer. Wise men seek Jesus! The Old Testament tells us that the "fear of the Lord is the beginning of wisdom," and we are to fear God and keep His commandments for that is the whole duty of man! The Bible also says we cannot make ourselves wise. "Neither make thyself over wise for why shouldst thou destroy thyself." There is a spiritual wisdom given to those who seek to know God and walk in obedience to His Word that is different from mere knowledge, for knowledge simply amasses and computes facts, whereas wisdom is the critical faculty that tells us what to do with them. According to the Bible, wisdom in the spiritual realm is more important than wisdom in any other area—physical, metaphysical, social, emotional, or scientific. What is the good of an astronaut knowing how to walk on the moon if his marriage is falling apart because he doesn't know how to walk on the earth?

There is another obvious reason for that statement. Only the spiritual realm goes on forever, and the writer of the book of Ecclesiastes says, quite rightly, all is foolish emptiness and folly if we don't put the most important thing first. In the Bible the world's wisdom is contrasted to the wisdom gained by seeking and coming to know Christ. The Bible tells us that the world, by its grand wisdom, decided there wasn't a God at all! It is then obvious that man's wisdom is less than the very foolishness of God! On the other hand, if foolish men will seek God, He will make them through Christ Himself in whom dwells all the treasures of wisdom and knowledge, so that, in Paul's words, we can have the very mind of Christ!

Matthew tells us of some wise men who appeared on the Christmas scene. The name he uses to describe them is Magi, which denotes one of a sacred caste, originally median, who apparently conformed to the Persian religion while retaining their old beliefs. In Matthew's account of the birth of Christ, the word is used in the plural telling us there were a number of such men who came from the East seeking Jesus. These were magicians with their own religion who would use drugs and medicines, spells and witchcraft, incantations and appeals to occult powers in their worship.

"Well" you say, "that's not very wise—I wouldn't do that—that's stupid!" Thousands of people would not agree with you today. They would say—"That's wise! That's just where it's at. I'm into astrology and reading my horoscope and dabbling in mind control meditation and even perhaps in white witchcraft!" Let me point something out to you. If you are seeking help and satisfaction in the stars and magical arts, there is a record of such people in Scripture; and if you would be as wise as they—and they were experts in the subject—then you will follow a star larger than everything in your sky and find it will lead you to the *Bright and Morning Star* wrapped up in baby bands and lying in a manger! "We have seen His star" those astrologer magicians said, and His star was so superior to anything else they had ever seen that they left all the rest to worship Him! How wise is wise? According to God's book, you are truly wise when you follow His star and no other.

But other religions have their wise men, too, you may argue. You can't say you have the only corner on the truth. But there is someone who said more than that! The Babe in the manger grew up to claim He not only spoke the truth or understood the truth, but that He was in very fact the Truth about the Truth! Christ's star is in essence the one Joseph of the Old Testament saw in his dream. All the other lesser stars of religion must bow down and worship His star! No other religion in the world claims the Incarnation of God. No other founder of religion ever came back from the dead to prove his point. No wonder the wise men, on alert by their own seeking hearts and finding a measure of truth in their own beliefs, followed and investigated a star that was shining bigger and brighter than any they had seen before!

Has there been a star in your sky yet? Something that has put you on alert to particular beliefs you have grown up with which are perhaps lacking? Is there something more to be found? The wise men began to seek for Jesus from just where they were; that's all we can expect anybody to do. Often we destroy people's interest by insisting they look at things from "our" position. If we could simply start from where they are and with what they've got to begin the journey

towards the Christ, we would see more people find and worship Him. For example, one thing the wise men believed from their own standpoint was that Christ was King of the Jews. It doesn't say anywhere they believed He was King of Heaven, but God started where they were with what they had and led them by the light on to the Light! If we build on the elements of truth we find already laid, we stand a good chance of seeing people complete their search in triumph. Whereas if we insist on finding all the areas of

controversy and arguing about them, we will, in all probability, see them return to their old beliefs.

I remember believing very firmly in evolution. When I lay in the hospital before I ever came to have faith in Christ, the girl in the next bed told me about the Bible being true. I asked her how she could possibly believe what it said when science had contradicted it—in the case of the theory of evolution. My search for God could well have stopped right there; I could easily have been turned back in my questioning to the mistaken belief that science was the savior of mankind; but instead of taking me head on and having a row, Janet simply pointed out that "science told us how the heavens go, but Jesus told us how to go to heaven." The Bible was not a scientific textbook, she said (which incidentally did not mean it was unscientific), but rather a book of the moral and spiritual realm which talked of our relationship with God. Such a wise answer helped me journey around the obstacle and eventually arrive at the manger!

Why, you may ask, do wise men want to find Jesus anyway? Surely it shows a weakness in a man's character if he needs something outside of himself to worship. We are made to be dependent. We depend on air to breathe, sleep, food, shelter, and a thousand and one emotional, psychological, and social things to be a healthy holistic person. We cannot live in total isolation. We are dependent on *somebody's* company—in fact, the harshest thing you can do to a man is to shut him up in solitary confinement. We depend on the elements for survival; the sunshine and the soft refreshing rain. We rely on some great unseen force to give us existence in the first place, and there is no man on earth who can keep himself alive. We are made to be dependent; and if this is so in all the areas of a man's life here, how much more in the spiritual and eternal realm. We are created to be spiritually dependent on someone greater than all of us. That is why wise men seek Jesus. They know, if they are at all observant human beings, that it is the nature of the creature called man to be dependent. The difference between the animals and man is simply the ability man has been given to be dependent spiritually. This is part of the dignity of the human being; for he is made to know God, and being thus made, seeks until he finds eternal rest.

When will wise men find Jesus, you may want to know? When did our scriptural searchers find Him? You remember the story. Having followed the star many miles to Jerusalem it disappeared, and they did the thing we probably would have done. They went straight to the top. The top, in this instance, was Herod, King of the Jews. If indeed the star they followed indicated a King was born for Israel, where else would He be found but in the King's palace? It was perfectly logical, but it was not perfectly spiritual! Big is not always best. The top is not always "where it is at." Man looks on the outward appearance, but the Lord looks in the heart, and the Magi could not see the evil murderous designs of Herod's heart. They believed his hypocritical words that he would like to worship the new King also, even though they must have wondered why the baby was *not* born in the palace to the ruling family! They were, however, to learn a very important lesson. Herod knew exactly where to go for

advice. He summoned the chief priests and scribes for a consultation, for he knew, evil though he was, where to go for the specific directions of the King's whereabouts—he needed to turn to the Scriptures! The wise men learned the star could only lead them so far; at this point they would have to turn to the Word of God to find their Savior. Having gathered the religious leaders together, Herod demanded of them where Christ would be born and they answered him, "In Bethlehem of Judah for thus it is written by the prophet. . . . And thou Bethlehem in the land of Judah are not the least among the Princes of Judah for out of thee shall come a Governor that shall rule my people Israel" (Matt. 3:5-6).

The Magi saw that stars can disappear, people are fallible, but the Bible is marvelously reliable; for hidden in the treasures of the Hebrew Scrolls lay the details of the birthplace of the King of Kings! There were secrets revealed there concerning the nation He would come from, the tribe, the family, and even the very town. There were even two Bethlehems, one in Judah and one in Zebulon; but God's Word was careful to indicate it would be Bethlehem Ephrata that would be honored by His Son's birth. Anyone can write history after the fact, but it takes a supernatural miracle of foreknowledge to write it in advance.

If I told you tonight at midnight a policeman would come to your door, I might be right or I might be wrong. If I then went on making wild guesses, giving you further information, I would stand more chance of making mistakes with the more details I gave you. The Old Testament insists on giving many details in advance concerning Christ's birth, life, and manner of death—and Jesus of Nazareth fulfilled every single one of them. Even if He had been afraid and had read those prophecies Himself and decided to hoax the world, it is hardly likely He could have organized the details of His birth! No, if wise men would search the Scriptures for proof of the divinity of the Babe of Bethlehem, they would find all the evidence they need that He was indeed the Lord's Christ. But then there are some foolish men who just pretend to seek Christ, like Herod, for example. His one motive was murderous jealousy. He was the puppet-king set up by the hated Romans to keep the Jews in order, despised by his

"Has their been a star in your sky yet?"

own. He had his reasons for seeking Christ, but he made sure they were well disguised. History tells us that Herod the Great increased the splendor of the temple at Jerusalem, but paid only lip service to the religion he professed. Cunningly he was able to deceive the wise men, pretending he, too, wished to bend the knee to the Messiah; but God knew his heart and hid Christ from his sight. The Bible says "You shall find Him when you shall seek for Him with *all* your heart," and the wise men sought Him like that. They left home and family and spent a fortune to find Him, and God moved the stars in heaven itself to make sure they did. Herod, on the other hand, only wanted to know the facts about Christ's birth so that he could get rid of Him. He was not able to see beyond his own personal selfishness. He knew that if this Child were allowed to live, He would be after his throne; and, refusing to consider any of the implications of his actions, he decided he didn't want to know anything more about Christ than the place of His birth! If he had allowed himself to examine the Messiah's message, he would have been called to repent of his sin, and that he was not prepared to do.

It was Aldous Huxley who said, "It's not that I *can't* believe—I *won't*, for I have motives for not wanting the world to have a meaning." His motive had to do with his *morals, not his mind!* The evidence is there, but the man who says his mind is made up—don't confuse him with the facts—has another problem than that of the intellect. Soren A. Kierkegaard, a wise man from Europe, sought Jesus. He said, "I confirmed through investigation, what I wanted to refute!" He, however, in contrast to Huxley was honest enough, having faced the conclusions, to believe that he had no alternative but commit himself to the proven facts of the Gospel.

Wise men still seek Jesus! When they find Him, the choice is theirs to kneel or to destroy. They cannot destroy the Christ for God will hide Him from them even as He hid Him from Herod all those thousands of years ago, disguising Him in a poor man's arms in swaddling bands and sheltering Him in a manger. But you can destroy yourself as Herod did. We don't know how many years it took those foreigners to search out the Christ Child, but it says in the Bible they dis-

covered Him in a house not a stable, and by that time He was a young child. It could have been another two years from the time they inquired in Jerusalem, for when Herod had waited that amount of time without their return to tell him where the Baby was, he lost his sanity, ordering his soldiers to kill all the male children under two years of age . . ."according to the time he had diligently inquired of the wise men."

The Magi were different. They had no scriptural background or Jewish advantage such as Herod had, only the light they had received. We are told we are to be judged by the light that we receive—not by the light we haven't received! For those with seeking hearts who respond to the little light they have, God will give more light until it leads them to the place where the young Child lies! The result of the wise men's search

was the reward of *exceeding great joy*, and so it will be for all who seek to worship Christ Jesus. But for Herod and those like him, what darkness lies ahead! Jesus said that dreadful judgment awaits those who as much as stumble a little child. He warned us that it were better that a millstone were fastened round the necks of such people and they were cast into the depths of the sea. What must await those like Herod who slaughter innocent babies or seek to kill the Christ Child all over again with their unbelief!

As the wise men came to the end of their mission and found Jesus the Savior, they sacrificed. They had carefully carried their most precious possessions with them, and now they laid them at His feet. Who knows, it may have been those very gifts that Joseph and Mary were able to utilize to escape into Egypt. Everything we give to Him, He receives and can use to fulfill His eternal plan. The Bible says the wise men were warned of Herod's evil intentions through a dream, and so they departed to their own country another way. We do not suppose they took back with them Jewish scrolls from the synagogue to help them in their newfound faith, but God gives the truly wise wisdom beyond themselves and their circumstances once they have found Jesus. A discernment of men's hearts and right decisions were granted to these men who knelt at His feet and whispered His name in loving adoration. Yes, the wise men departed into their country another way. Not only did they journey back to their homes on a new path, they journeyed back as new men! "If any man be in Christ, he is a new creation, old things are passed away, behold all things are become new," says the sacred Scriptures.

It's true—it's all true! So how wise is wise? According to Solomon, the "wisest" of men: "The fear of the Lord is the beginning of knowledge, but fools despise wisdom and instruction (Prov. 1:7) . . . So incline thine ear unto wisdom, and apply thine heart to understanding; Yea, if thou criest after knowledge, and liftest up thy voice for understanding; If thou seekest her as silver, and searchest for her as for hidden treasures; Then shalt thou understand the fear of the Lord, and find the knowledge of God (Prov. 2:2-5). *Wise men still seek Jesus!*

*"Old age, when lent the Spirit's intelligence,
knows when to open its mouth."*

Never Say Never

Have you noticed how old age and youth hold hands? It's the most natural thing in the world to see Grandma cuddling her newborn grandchild as she sits in her rocking chair! And did you ever notice how many *old* people featured in the action when that *very* special Babe arrived that first Christmas? Was it that God knew He could trust the elderly with wisdom's right reactions? There was old, sick Simeon, Zacharias and Elisabeth— well advanced in age—and widowed Anna, too. Christ came to each and made the difference. What difference?

First there was Simeon waiting for the consolation of Israel. He had been patient for so long, I can imagine he must have begun to wonder if he had mistaken the Spirit's message to his heart, that he would not die until he had seen the Lord's Christ. Perhaps he would *never* live to see the day after all, he thought. But Simeon was to learn you *never say never,* for having walked into the temple and been strangely alerted by God that the tiny baby in Mary's arms was Divinity Himself come to console the Israel he loved, he knew he was ready to die at last. Old age is not always so ready to depart. Perhaps that is because old age is not always sure where it is departing to; and if you are not sure of that, it is understandable that fear reigns!

Are you sick and old, and frightened that you are going to die? Maybe you have been looking for some consolation for a long time and have found little or none. Just where have you been looking I wonder? Did you know you need to look into the face of the Babe of Bethlehem and *see* God's salvation for yourself, then embracing Him, you will be ready to depart? "But what consolation can the Lord's Christ bring to my old age?" you may ask. Firstly, He can bring the comfort of forgiveness. The Christ can help the guilt that sits so hotly in your flushed cheeks as you think of "this" or "that" you did and never got to mend. He will forgive the act, the thought, the lousy motivation, or the sly manipulation, even the lack of understanding you displayed. He will blot out from heaven's mind the unsaid word of love withheld in punishment, or the endless worrying about the things you did or didn't do. All, all can be forgiven; for when you hold onto God's Savior, you can, like Simeon, depart this life in peace.

Secondly, Christ can bring to old age the consolation that you are not alone. Simeon was an old man, a righteous man—and a full man! He was *full* of the Holy Ghost. While Jesus walked in Galilee, He never left His disciples alone. One day He told them He would have to go away and they

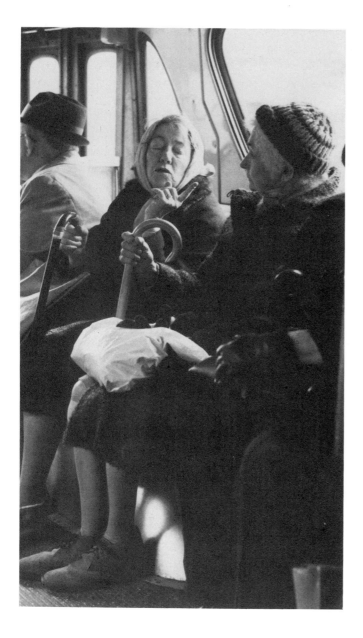

Thirdly, Christ can bring to old age the consolation that a new body awaits us in the next life. Perhaps you feel like the old man who, when asked how he was today, replied "I'm fine, but the house that I live in is badly in need of repair!" When the Lord's Christ needed a body to be the vehicle of His actions among us, God prepared one for Him, and He used it for thirty-three years to "flesh" out the character of the Eternal One. When Christ dismissed *His Spirit* from the cross into His Father's hands, other hands were there to take *His body* from the tree and wrap it up for death. But after three days God raised up that very *same body to give us consolation!* What comfort to know that God can raise the dead and will raise up our bodies to be like His glorious One! The Jews believed in the resurrection of the dead; and Simeon, being the devout Jew that he was, knew it would be the Messiah that would make that possible. Can you imagine what that old man was thinking as he gazed with his own eyes upon His salvation, not only salvation for his soul, but for his old sick tired body as well! Now he could *depart* and be at peace which was far, far better!

Not long ago I visited a hospital where I had been asked to give a speech at a fund-raising dinner for a new birthing wing and a hospice, a place where terminally ill patients could be helped to die with dignity. "Let's go and see the birthing wing first," suggested my host. I asked him "Which one?" seeing that they really had two; the baby birthing wing which was the entrance to *this* life and the hospice which was the birthing wing to the next!

As Simeon held the baby Christ in his arms, he knew his time to be born into eternity had arrived! What heavenly delight must that old man's countenance have displayed.

Old age wears many faces. It can wear the furrowed frown of disappointment, as well as the delicious dawn of delight—like the faces of Zacharias and Elisabeth, for example. They couldn't help being a little disappointed, for their prayers had not been answered. For years they had prayed for a child and the child had not been given. To reach the climax of one's life with *some* prayers unanswered seems reasonable enough, but this had been no ordinary request. A childless couple were treated with sad pity in that age and

would not be able to follow Him where He was going. Not then anyway. Later when *their* work was done they would follow, but not yet. They were devastated when He told them, but He spoke comforting words to them, promising He would send a "Consoler" so they would never be lonely again. The Comforter would be one exactly the same as He, and would be called the "Paraclete" which means one called alongside to help. He would actually come to live "in them" and not just be physically by their side. Simeon had known the comfort of the Spirit before he met Christ, but now his joy was full.

culture, for who would carry on the family name? Now it seemed that prayer would *never* be answered for they were *very* old. But Christ was coming into the situation and Elisabeth was to learn when that happens you *never say never!*

Do you face some impossible dreams saying *never* this Christmastime? Perhaps you feel too old, too sick, too weak, or too disappointed with God to bother asking Him *again* about whatever it was He didn't seem to bother about *last* time you stormed heaven's gates! Maybe you would have reacted as Zacharias did when the angel appeared to him and said, "Your prayer is answered. . . ." I can see the old man now, casting furiously about in his mind for a clue as to that particular puzzle! Which prayer, he must have wondered? His prayer for the people he was pastoring subjected to the tyranny of Rome? Or perhaps he meant the prayers he had prayed for the hypocritical Pharisees who make godly Zacharias sometimes ashamed to be a Jew! Or maybe the angel was

referring to some of those prayers of his for his own waning health? Before his thoughts had come home to a satisfactory conclusion, God's messenger completed his message. "Fear not, Zacharias, for thy prayer is heard and *thy wife Elisabeth shall bear thee a son* and thou shalt call his name John!" *That prayer!* Why, that was the most out-of-date prayer of them all! When he and Elisabeth had reached old age, they had accepted the fact *that prayer* had been dealt with; it had been answered by an emphatic *no!* To begin with there were so many "natural" circumstances that had answered the prayer. Their bodies were past the normal age when reproduction could take place, but they needed to be reminded that prayer doesn't deal in natural situations but in *supernatural* dynamics *in* natural situations! Then again, that particular petition had been presented so very regularly with no visible results, they had become a little uncomfortable about praying on and on about it anymore. They knew God wasn't

deaf; He must have heard and chosen to answer with a loud silence, and so losing heart they had decided to stop. Yes, that particular request was almost forgotten; it had been so long since it had been prayed. But God delights to keep some of His choicest answers for old age. Some surprises are stored in heaven's memories for a time when others may forget we need surprises.

So often I hear old people say, "I've nothing left to live for, because I've nothing left to look forward to." But you do! You can start and expect the sunrise surprises of God! If you'll take heart and listen for the angel telling you "your prayer is heard," He will come to you! Sit still and let him visit your mind and remind you of the past. Then start and count your blessings, one by one. Then you may realize the things you count are really answered prayers you've long forgotten you ever even prayed. I don't consider myself to be old, being probably only half the age of Zacharias and Elisabeth, and yet I am already seeing my children grow and develop in ways that carry me back to remembrances of prayer around their cots. Prayers that were heard and are just beginning to be answered! I remember, when our children were but infants, asking God to help them in the future to walk tall and straight whenever peers would pressure them to let down the standards they had raised. Not very long ago as one came home early from a party and gave us her reasons, I heard the angel say "Your prayer is heard!" Which prayer? The prayer of yesteryear!

Another day not too long ago I sat upon a plane. We had just been fed and watered and laid down to sleep. The air was still, the flight was smooth. Then suddenly without any warning whatsoever, the whole machine dropped hundreds of feet, sucked into a downdraft as occasion sometimes has it! It was certainly the worst turbulance I had ever experienced and as it continued for some minutes, I glanced sideways at my terrified companion and thought briefly of yet another prayer I had prayed eight years previously. It had been a desperate frantic scream for help as I, too, had clutched the airplane seat and faced the unthinkable thoughts that bumped and jerked along with the rhythm of the plane into my frightened mind. "Please God," I had pled desperately, "take away this *awful* fear of flying."

I smiled at my companion and patted his arm saying "It's OK—it's just a bit bumpy," and, oh, how my heart rejoiced, for I *never* dreamed the time would come when I wouldn't be one bit scared; *somewhere* I heard the angel say *"never say never"* — your prayer is answered." Yes, it helps while we are waiting a long time for a very important request to be dealt with, to look around our lives a little, and count the answers to past petitions we have not taken time to recognize.

Living with your own deep disillusionments is one thing, but coping with other people's disappointments is another! Many a night as Elisabeth stayed at home alone, she must have grappled with the memories of her husband's intense desire for a son. She couldn't have helped feeling that in some sense she was responsible. There would have been the family's and neighbors' expectations, too, that would have needed to be faced. Do you identify with Elisabeth?

Are you old and disappointed? Have the "beating years" brought you to your knees in angry remonstrations against God? Do you feel you're unwanted and unloved—or perhaps even unlovely? Maybe you were once beautiful, and now you spend your meager income on cosmetic ploys for decorated age. Have you not learned as yet that no chemist on earth can decorate disappointment into delight! Do you say desperately to yourself, "I'll never be needed again"? *Never say never.* Perhaps you have been disappointed in the past, but remember Zacharias and Elisabeth and think how often God paints His choicest colors in His latest sunsets! God will bring color into your existence against the darkening sky; if you only dare to believe. He will do something new for you. Think about Elisabeth. Didn't He work out something fresh for her, bringing new vitality into her old body? Elisabeth's greatest opportunity came to her at the end of her life, not the beginning or the middle of it. Not only did Zacharias, who had been temporarily struck dumb through doubt, need her, but Mary, young, frightened, and tragically misunderstood, would find valuable encouragement and affirmation through her loving care.

One of the things that must have been the hardest for Mary to cope with must have been her family's refusal to accept her account of the

"God paints His choicest colors in His latest sunsets."

miraculous conception. When Joseph decided to break their engagement, she must have thought if she couldn't convince *him*, she would *never* convince anybody. *Never say never!* God knew Elisabeth would not only believe her, but would be in herself a living example of miraculous conception! Like the youth of today, the youth of yesterday needed the elderly to reinforce their faith. You need *never* think there is nothing left for you to do. Ask God to send you children to encourage, for this modern world's restive, seeking youth need the solid safety of aged faith!

Then there was Anna. Anna was a widow and had been so for eighty-four years. Seven years after her wedding day she was drastically reduced to the most vulnerable status of a woman alone. The other day I was intrigued to read an article entitled "Teach Your Wife How to Be a Widow." It considered some thought-provoking facts, such as "most American wives outlive their husbands" and "today's average wife will be a widow for ten years and many face longer periods of widowhood." This book—as suggested in the foreword—should prove of value to the numerous breed of American men who work their fingers to the bone throughout their lives, yet fail to prepare their marriage partner to handle the wealth they will bequeath them and their children!

I know another book that will prove useful

to widows. It will prepare them to handle the other bequests of widowhood, like loneliness, bitterness, despair, guilt, and self-pity. It is called the Bible. It tells of widows so those of us who read these pages and are celebrating a happy family life may not bury our heads in the sand and say, "Not me," but simply and more realistically say, "Not yet," and begin to equip ourselves to be one of the possible ten million widows in the U.S.A. "But it will never happen to me," you say—*never say never!* I'm sure Anna never believed it would happen to her, and so soon! To be a young widow is one thing, but to be widowed until such a great age is another!

But Anna knew where the answer was to be found. She departed not from the temple, but served God night and day! It would have been very easy for her to depart, not only from the temple, but also from her faith in the God who had allowed this terrible thing to happen to her. But Anna *departed not!* Accepting the reality of her husband's death, she filled the void by service of another nature.

Acceptance and service—one a submission to the cold facts and finality of the relationship

down here on earth, and the other an active losing of oneself in other people's problems—can bring a measure of relief in our bereavements. When these things had been practiced, Christ met Anna in the temple and brought her consolation. Not only did meeting Christ cause her to give thanks, but God gave her a special privilege, using her to tell others about Him. Can you imagine becoming an evangelist and starting a whole new ministry at the age of eighty-five? "No, I can't," you say. "I could never speak to people about my faith. I find it difficult now, and if I ever reach the age of eighty-five, I would doubtless find it impossible!" *Never say never. Anna spoke of Him to all who looked for* redemption in Jerusalem! She didn't get out on the street corners and start to preach. Somehow God alerted her to the ones who were seeking release and help, and who would be open to her words. "What wisdom and discernment," you say. *Old age, when lent the Spirit's intelligence, knows when to open its mouth!*

And so we've thought about Simeon, Zacharias, Elisabeth, and Anna. Old age consoled by Christ at Christmastime. And then there is *you.* "Oh, but I could *never, . . . "* you say. *Never say never.*

"He that is mighty hath done to me great things and Holy is His name" (Luke 1:46).

The Sweet Peas
of Christmas

When I lived in England and wanted to lift someone's spirits, I would gather a bunch of those delicious sweet peas that clambered in a profusion of color up the trellis outside our cottage and present them, with the happy knowledge of the "lift" they would bring sitting jauntily on a kitchen cabinet or dining-room table. Let me gather a bunch of sweet peas of another kind and present them to those of you who lack a little color in your lives this Christmastime.

The first sweet "P" is the *Peace* promised by the angels to the shepherds. This was not to be a peace between the nations, for Christ Himself would tell us that nation would rise against nation, and wars and rumors of wars would continue until He came again. He was not speaking of peace in the family, either, for the angel knew that many who would follow Christ would encounter hostility from "foes" in their very own household. In fact, the King of Peace was to say, "I come not to bring peace, but a sword!" Now that seems to be a real contradiction; how could that be? The angel told of God's Peace *toward* men. God was offering mankind a cessation of hostilities, for He had found a way to end the war! What war? The Bible teaches us that man is at "enmity" with God. He rebelled against the King and ran away to try and find another kingdom in which to live. At Christmas the grand offer of amnesty was announced from heaven—peace from God—on His terms, in His way, to forgiven offenders who would be willing to say they were sorry. But all people would not take advantage of the peace that was offered, and those who did would find themselves attacked by those who didn't! Even in a single family unit, one would receive and one reject God's gracious gift; and it would be just as He had said—like a dividing sword between mother and daughter, father and son, mother-in-law and daughter-in-law. But peace between God and man is His purpose for mankind. He instigated and made it all possible, and we need to remind ourselves of the fact that He didn't need to have a Christmas at all. That's why the angels sang "Glory to God," not glory to man! He could well have sent a child of judgment to that manger with an express order to destroy us, but He didn't send a punishment-child; He sent a Peace-Child! What a beautiful flower.

The second sweet "P" I would collect and present to you is the "P" that stands for *Promise*. The pledges of God are many and varied in their colors, and we see them especially in all their vivid beauty at Christmastime. The first thing about the promises of God concerns His grand ability to make and keep His word. We are dealing here with the *ability* of the promiser to come through. When Stuart and I were in full-time youth work, my husband "promised" me that one day we would all get on a big plane, fly to Spain and bask in the sun. I knew he was willing, but I also knew, because I'd seen our bank balance, he wasn't able! One day he came home and told me it was all going to come to pass, just as he had told me, because *"Norman said so."* Norman was a dear, generous, *wealthy* friend of ours who had been very good to us in the past. "You pray; I'll pack," I said, dashing upstairs, knowing if Norman said so, Norman was not only willing, but was also *able!* Likewise, we are encouraged to believe that

God is able to keep His promises to us, because of the ones He has already kept. Think of Mary, told that she would bear a child miraculously, without the instrumentality of a human father. That was a mighty big statement to make; but Mary sang after it had occurred just as the angel had said it would, "He that IS MIGHTY hath done to me great things and Holy is His name." All of God's character lies behind His word. He cannot lie; He cannot deceive us; for He *is holiness and truth* and will perform what He has promised, for He *is eternal ability.* Having been reminded of the vows God has kept in the past, we can then begin to *dare to trust Him now.* He that acts out of His ability proves His credibility.

Don Richardson, a missionary to the Sawis in New Guinea—men, women, and children still living in the Stone Age—found himself among headhunting cannibals who used skulls of their victims as pillows! They idealized treachery, and "fattened with friendship" those they planned on having for dinner. When Don preached the Gospel to them, they rejected Jesus and made Judas their hero! Then one day Don found, from their very own culture, the illustration he needed to reach them. His tribe was in a continual state of war with the people around them, and two of the tribes met to talk of peace. One of the men took his own little boy and, with agonized tears, gave him into the arms of the enemy. This little one was to be the "peace" child that the receiving tribe was to take as their own and raise with love and care as best they knew how. They would be watched carefully (from a distance) by the sacrificing father. Both tribes knew the war would immediately resume if ever the little one was abused, fell sick, or died! The promise of peace was not enough—the credibility of the promise depended on the action of the father and leader who made it, for the receiving tribe would *have to know* that a man who would actually give up his own son into the arms of his enemies could be trusted indeed! After observing this ritual, it was not hard at all for Don Richardson to present the story of the One who had given up His only Son as "Peace-Child" to a hostile tribe called man, knowing for certain they would crucify Him. Surely a Father so intent on making peace could be trusted after that!

The next thing we need to gather from our bunch of sweet "P's" concerning the promises of God has to do with His *Fidelity*. That means His absolute faithfulness, for what He has done once He will do again. He cannot change—for a change presupposes something better or worse, and God has been revealed as total perfection. In other words, the angel still appears in our sky and lights up our dark horizon, demanding our attention and promising us God's words are as powerful and credible today as 2,000 years ago! God's messages of hope are for you and for me and were not only intended for a bunch of shepherds, a handful of wise men, and an innkeeper! They are valid today because God's word abides forever. "Heaven and earth shall pass away," said Jesus, "but my word shall *never* pass away."

Usually the promises of people die with them. I remember telling our parents we were giving up a lucrative career and going into the Christian ministry; and I recollect my father promising Stuart and I that, while he lived, he would see to it we should never want. He knew he could not promise us his care and provision after he died, for the simple reason he would not be around to see to it. Jesus can continually come through on *His* promises, however, for He didn't die to die—He died to live in the power of an endless life.

The next sweet "P" has to do with *Performance!* What will it take, you may ask, to unlock the good of God's promises to me? It will take my active belief! When Mary ran to the hill country to tell Elisabeth what had happened to her, Elisabeth sang her a song—"Blessed be *she that believed,"* she sang, *"for there shall be a performance* of those things which were told *her* from the Lord" (Luke 1:45). Mary had not only believed God *could,* she had been convinced that God *would* do those things He had told her. Faith isn't believing God can, but expecting that God will—and there's a difference. This does not mean we can expect God to do any old thing we ask Him to; it means we can expect Him to do the things He has *already said* He will do for us *according to His Word!* Are the things we expect of God promised to us in His Word? Some people get very cross with the Almighty because He hasn't come through with the things we *think He should have promised!* Maybe we asked Him to make us successful or popular, or requested a Cadillac or some material thing. He told us we could hope for our daily bread, not daily caviar! We need to begin to read the Bible and see for what we *can* believe God. When we find the things He would have us expect, then we can claim them and be confident that what He has promised He is able, also, to perform.

Another sweet "P" that we can pick from the angel's bouquet is *Praise.* This was an extra-large blossom, I am sure. "Glory to God," the angels sang! What does it mean to praise God? To worship means to ascribe "worth" to Him; in fact, the word could be written "worthship." When we involve ourselves in praise, we are saying that God is worth something to us. He is worth my attention, my time, my adoration, my loving service. As Mary burst forth into her *Magnificent Magnificat,* she taught us some lessons in praise. "My soul magnifies the Lord," she said; for as far as Mary was concerned, her personality was simply to be a magnifying glass, making the Lord bigger than herself! This is praise. We can always check up if our whole personhood is involved in the business of bringing glory to God by asking ourselves the question, "What image am I projecting? Who do others see as larger than life when I am in conversation at a party, or in a school situation, or when I am taking responsibility on some committee or other?" Just who is

"My soul doth magnify the Lord" (Luke 1:46).

being magnified? To worship means to believe *He* is worth magnifying more than *me*, although this is not to say I am worth nothing. The language of humility says I am worth something because of God, and I want my wholehearted attitude to magnify the One who gave me worth! Mary's soul was *transparent* and brought glory to God. Mary's spirit was *triumphant*. "My spirit has rejoiced in God my Savior," she sang. Mary, too, needed a Savior and here she acknowledges that very fact. She sings of *"my* Savior" and indicates He is the source of her joy. Now remember she didn't have too much to be joyful about. With a broken engagement — "shattered dreams, wounded heart, and broken toys"—as the song has it, she shouldn't have felt like singing at all. But joy is an altogether different thing than happiness. My husband says that happiness depends on happenings, and if your happenings happen to happen the way you happen to want them to happen—you're happy! Joy means you're happy anyway—*whatever happens.* To have a tri-

umphant spirit means you sing in the midst of sorrow, bring glory to God and magnify the Lord who causes such rejoicing. He promised in the Book of Isaiah that He would give us "the garment of praise for the spirit of heaviness;" and Mary, wrapped in such happy robes, sang praise in the midst of pain. Maybe some of you are grappling with an unbelieving husband just as Mary did, and you wonder if he will ever believe as you do. How can he ever come to faith, you wonder, when he doesn't even go to church? Your body is the "temple" of the Holy Spirit and "church" has come to him; for as he watches you at worship—rejoicing in sorrow and singing in the rain—then your soul will be magnifying the Lord and he will be seeing Him clearly whether he tells you he does or not. Mary could honestly say that her Christmas was without peace, but *not without the Peace-Child,* and *that's* what made the difference. God doesn't expect us to praise Him for the awful things that happen, but for His help in the midst of those grim circumstances.

The last sweet "P" we will pick is *Presence.* "How can I know all this in reality?" you may ask. "It all sounds so idealistic; and, anyway, Mary was Mary and I am just little old me, struggling and failing and certainly not made to be a heroine." Let's go back to the angel's interview with Mary. In Luke's Gospel, after being told she will conceive a child, Mary asks the angel, "How shall this be, seeing I know not a man?" It was an obvious question and spoke of her willing realization that there was no way on earth she could understand what would happen to her unless God gave the explanation along with the promise. The angel answered and said unto her, "The Holy Ghost shall come upon thee and the power of the Most High shall overshadow thee." That was how! The Holy Ghost would "shadow over" her. What is a shadow? According to the dictionary a shadow is one's inescapable attendant or companion. When, then, does this supernatural overshadowing occur? Whenever we come to understand the principle and appropriate the power.

What is the principle that we have to understand and put into operation? It is first a yielding! "Behold the handmaid of the Lord," said Mary. It is a submissive, serving attitude that says, *"Be it unto me according to Thy word."* God will never ask us to do what Mary did, but He may well ask us to live with a difficult man, or minister to an aging parent, or cope with the pressures of temptation; and it is in such times we need to ask Him to do for us what we *cannot* do for ourselves. Then He will overshadow us and be our inescapable attendant and companion. His presence will give us the strength to do the impossible, for as Mary sang, "He hath showed *strength* with His arm." Remembering all that the Almighty had done in the past when "He hath holpen his servant Israel," she reminded herself that now He "would holpen her, too!"

"Holpen" is a good old-fashioned word meaning "helped," but it was just the word I needed to hear one Christmastime not very long ago. I remember praying earnestly for some heavenly "holpen," as I was to be rushed into hospital for surgery, and for that I needed a song! He gave me one, too, the words of which were, "Thou wilt keep him in perfect peace whose mind is stayed on Thee." "Oh Lord, my heart is fixed in

Thee," I read in response and realized I must do the fixing of my heart on Him, then trust Him with the fixing of the circumstances. Can you believe I had a song in my heart as they wheeled me to the operating theater? I could hardly believe it myself, but it is true, because I was intensely aware of the overshadowing of that inescapable Presence. Maybe you think it presumptuous to claim the power He gave to Mary for yourself. Don't think like that. Mary herself said, for our encouragement, "The One who can do all things has done great things for me—Oh, Holy is His name—*truly His mercy rests on those who fear Him in every generation!*" That means *you* and that means me!

So let me present you with a bunch of sweet "P's" and remind you of the beautiful bouquet of Christmas flowers the angel brought for all of us—Peace, Promise, Praise, Performance, and the very Presence of God Himself. What a *magnificent magnificat* each one of us has to sing *if* we take the gifts God offers and worship Him!

"Fear not, for, behold, I bring you tidings of great joy which shall be to all people" (Luke 2:10).

"Fear Not!"

It's funny what people are frightened about. I have been frightened most of my life! When I was a very little girl I was frightened of the enemy airplanes that kept dropping bombs all over my life. Then I was afraid I would never be as beautiful as my sister. I was very afraid of the shadows that chased away my sleep at night when I was all alone in my little pink and white bedroom; and I was frightened my father didn't love me as much as I wanted him to. As I grew up, my fears grew right along with me; and the bigger I got, the larger they loomed.

When I was a teenager I was afraid I'd get short boyfriends (I was tall); then I was afraid I wouldn't get *any* boyfriends. Then I was frightened my best friend, who was very pretty, would steal any boyfriend I managed to get! I was frightened I wouldn't graduate from school, and I was very much afraid if I did, I would not know what to do afterward. When I got to college, I was afraid I couldn't compete; and I was frightened all the other girls would have nicer clothes. Then I was afraid I wouldn't like the children I was given to teach, and I was frightened they wouldn't remember what I'd taught them!

When I became engaged, I was frightened something awful would happen to Stuart or me before the wedding day and we would never get married at all! Once I was married, I was fearful my husband would die from my cooking, or choke on some meat! When I found out I was pregnant I was ever so afraid I'd produce a mongoloid child, or if a normal one, it would die of crib death. As three children came along, I was frightened they would grow up to reject God, or go on drugs, or leave home. When they arrived at teen age, I was scared out of my mind if they were ever five minutes late coming home from school. I wondered if they'd been raped or kidnapped or attacked. When the time came for them to get married, I was afraid they'd choose the wrong partners who would dread having me as their mother-in-law.

I have discovered I don't have to wait until I'm old to finish being afraid. I have found out I can be old already if I continue practicing fear instead of faith; it is quite possible to be paralyzed with fears which age you prematurely. I have already been afraid of the far-distant future, expecting calamities and catastrophies galore, right up to the time I am sure I will be left to rot in some awful old-folks' home, where I am already afraid no one will ever come to visit me! It's *funny* what some people are afraid of! That is unless the "some people" is *you, and then it isn't funny at all!*

Having been afraid *all* of my life of bad, dark,

horrible things—real or imaginary—and believing none could be as scared as I, it came as somewhat of a shock to discover the people in the Christmas story were afraid, too. Now some of their anxiety I could understand. I would have been afraid of being pregnant at the ripe old age of eighty if I'd been Elisabeth—or at tender teen age if I'd been Mary! I'd have been scared to marry a pregnant girl if I'd been Joseph; and I'm sure I'd have been worried I'd been a fool spending all my money on some wild-goose chase if I'd been the wise men. I would also have been terrified of the Roman soldiers stealing my sheep or torturing me just for the fun of it, if I'd been a shepherd boy. But the people in the Bible story weren't just afraid of *those* sort of things. They were afraid of things you wouldn't expect them to be afraid of at all—

like God, His messengers, and His glory! Now *that's* strange! Take Zacharias, for example. There he was busy praying. He'd prayed regularly *all* his life, but suddenly he had one prayer answered, and that scared him out of his wits. You *can* get scared about that, you know! Some of you reading these pages would drop dead with shock if God answered any of your prayers, and maybe that is because you have not really been expecting Him to, because it has seemed presumptuous of you to ask God to do more than bend an eternal ear! Well, blessed is he that expecteth nothing, for he shall not be disappointed! It's an awesome thing when God moves into your prayer life and actually says something back! Most of the time He doesn't have a chance to say anything much, because too often we barge rudely into His presence with our

54

heavenly shopping list, as long as our arm, and act as though we'll get a parking ticket if we don't collect the goods and split! At other times, we don't expect a literal answer at all, as if God is limited to spiritual things and is helpless concerning material substances; as if He never did tell us to pray: "Give us this day our daily bread."

One day Peter was in prison. The local Christians met in a home to pray for him, no doubt asking God to release him from jail. God did! Peter was a little bit bewildered when he came to outside the prison gates, but soon he realized he had been miraculously delivered and decided to head for the place he knew the believers were having their midweek prayer meeting. They were praying all right, but they could well be described as unbelieving believers; for

when he knocked on the door and told them he had arrived, Rhoda, the girl who ran to see who it was, thought he was a ghost. She actually left him standing outside while she relayed this bit of information to the others, thinking perhaps he could dispense with locks and bolts if he were a spook! In other words, she did *not* expect a literal answer to the prayers that had been prayed. Prayer is simply the speaking part of our relationship with God, and God's side of the conversation is often neglected, or His promises are not taken seriously at all. Can you imagine the holy fear that would fill our hearts if we actually began to believe that God meets us in prayer and is willing to say "Yes!" Prayer is "a place to meet" and the Bible says "he that cometh to God must believe that He is, and that *He is a Rewarder* of

"Fear not . . . for thou hast found favor with God" (Luke 1:30).

those who diligently seek Him!" The Scriptures also tell us succinctly, *"Ye have not because ye ask not."*

Let's think about Joseph for a moment. Joseph was frightened to marry Mary; and the angel came and told him not to be, saying to him, "Joseph, thou son of David, fear not to take unto thee Mary thy wife, for that which is conceived in her is of the Holy Ghost." It's a funny thing that some men can actually be frightened of their wife's relationship with God! I know a lot of people who get married without giving God too much thought on their wedding day. He is really not part of their ongoing reckoning. Oh, I don't mean they don't get married in a church; they do, but if they were honest they would tell us that's only because of some religious superstition, or the parents wish it, or because the church building lends itself to a romantic sort of setting for the photographs! Then the wife enters into this intimate relationship with God and has something going spiritually that cuts the husband right out of the picture. She may try to explain it all, but sometimes he can't understand what on earth she's talking about, and it doesn't make much sense anyway, not to a pragmatic, down-to-earth mate like him! It's quite understandable that he's frightened and confused as he now finds himself married to a girl he didn't marry; and feeling somehow betrayed, he more often than not decides to fight it out or else ignore the whole thing and hope it will go away! How strange that any man should be fearful of his wife's relationship with God! If he thinks the thing through he must realize she can *only* be a better wife, a more loving lover, and a more mothering mother than ever before. He stands to gain all the way; for God is good, and God is love, and God is purity, as well as a lot of other marvelous things. What man in his right mind would object to his wife being good, loving, and pure? Yes, it's funny what people are frightened about!

Then there were the shepherds. Now I can imagine those rough-and-ready men being frightened of wolves, lions, and bears—even the dark! But it's funny what some men are frightened about. They were scared of angels and bright lights, and a Word directly from heaven! "And, lo, an angel of the Lord came upon them, and the glory of the Lord shone round about them, and they were *very much afraid*. And the angel said unto them, Fear not; for, behold, I bring you good tidings of great joy, which shall be to all people. For unto you is born this day in the city of David, a Savior Who is Christ the Lord" (Luke 2:9-11).

How can anyone be afraid of good news? The angel had to emphasize *that* point. It's a *good* message we bring to you, they said. Don't be afraid of it, for it will bring you *great joy*. Many people I know won't read the Word of God because it frightens them. They like to have a Bible in the house to scare the devil away, but it scares *them* away, too! They are frightened of its archaic English, or its tiny print and its technical jargon. They are fearful someone, somewhere, has proven it wrong, or science has written it all off, or biblical scholars have ripped it to shreds; and they are fearful they could never make sense of it anyway if the "experts" are fighting tooth and nail over this and that. So they live in the night and stick to what they know, abiding in their familiar fields, keeping watch over their flocks. They do their job and treat folk as right as they know how and believe if they do their best it will all work out in the end! But look at the transformation in these men's lives when the message burst through and they got over their fear and said to each other "Let *us* now *go* and *see* this thing that has come to pass!" Maybe you are like the shepherds, and if only you would open your Bible and read the good news for yourself, you would discover it would bring you *great joy*. If you would realize the Lord will make known unto *you* the things concerning Jesus and clarify the truth so you can really understand, you would find He'll lead you to read in the right place in the Bible at just the right time. Like the shepherds, you would go back to your fields new men, glorifying and praising God for all the things you've heard and seen *as it has been told unto you!*

When I first opened my Bible, I didn't know which way up it should be! I didn't know where to start, so I started at the beginning in the Book of Genesis—and buried myself in Leviticus! I knelt down and prayed, asking God to show me where to look for some good news that would bring some joy to my joyless life. I noticed the books were listed in orderly

sections like a huge library. There was a history section, a place for autobiographies, poetry, then wisdom, literature and a set of books called the Gospels from which I could learn about the Lord Jesus Christ. Then I discovered that the Epistles taught me how I could follow the Jesus I could see in the Gospels, and the Book of Revelation showed me how it would all end when we had followed Him all the way to heaven. God's Spirit lit up my mind as brightly as the angels lit up the darkness over Bethlehem's hills, and He chased away my fears that I could not understand. Don't be frightened of investigating the good news for yourself—even as the shepherds did.

Then there was Mary. Yes, even Mary was frightened. "And the angel came in unto her, and said, 'Hail, thou who art highly favored, the Lord is with thee; blessed art thou among women.' And when she saw him, *she was troubled* at his saying and considered in her mind what manner of greeting this could be. And the angel said unto her, *'Fear not, Mary;* for thou hast found favor with God'" (Luke 1:28-30). What was she frightened about? The angel conveyed the heavenly message to her that she was *highly favored,* which set her casting about in her mind why he had addressed her so; and as she pondered the mystery, deeply perturbed, he repeated his greeting, "Fear not Mary, *for thou hast found favor with God!"* It's funny what people are frightened about. Mary was troubled when she heard she pleased the Lord! The word that was used by the angel implies grace. Mary had found grace and favor; and while grace is a free gift, favor may be deserved or gained! The virgin graced by God, chosen to bear His Son, had highly deserved the Almighty's blessing. Young though she was, she had already proven her faithfulness in loving service. It's funny the things that frighten people.

I know some marvelous folk who love the Lord and are wonderfully gifted by God. They hold positions of responsibility in society and the church they serve and have truly gained favor, not only in man's eyes, but in the Father's sight as well. It is to *these* sort of people that God often offers the opportunities of His highest calling— there may be some missionary endeavor or some second mile, some mighty work, something above or beyond the call of duty. Knowing the sort of men and women God is looking for causes many to hold back in case the Lord *highly favors* them with such a costly opportunity of service! They may have started well—beginning to run the race that has been set before them; but as they become aware that God is calling for a *full* commitment and, like Mary, they have a choice in the matter, they back off, frightened of the consequences of full surrender!

During His earthly ministry, Jesus had many such disciples. At one point, His sayings got tougher and the lines were clearly drawn. It was all or nothing, and we read that at that point, "Some went back and walked no more with Him!" Don't be afraid to kneel and echo Mary's prayer of faith and obedience that chased away her fears: "Behold the slave of the Lord—*be it unto me according to Thy word.*"

Yes, it's funny what people are frightened of. They are frightened of death and darkness, disease and demons, but frightened more by deliverance, delight, and determination to be fully involved with the Christ Child! *Be wise,* for the fear of the Lord is the beginning of wisdom. To fear God properly doesn't mean to be frightened of Him, as you are frightened of those other things we have been talking about; but to so reverence Him, you yield to His will, being more "afraid" of displeasing Him than anything else.

Fear Him ye saints
and you will then have nothing else to fear;
make you His service, your delight,
your wants shall be His care!

So be wise—
swap fear for faith—
and rejoice!

". . . and thou shalt conceive in thy womb—and bring forth a Son!" (Luke 1:31).

"Congratulations, You're a Woman!"

So said Gabriel, and he said it to a woman! He told Mary that a "Holy Thing" should be born of her and should be called the Son of God. So much is being said today about the woman's person, place, profession, and pay! In so many ways in the past, women have had a bad deal; and even in this day and age, in many countries a woman is looked upon as definitely inferior.

A story is told of a visitor to a certain country before World War II. He was a little taken aback to see the man of the household strutting ahead of a troup of women carrying all his parcels on their heads, as they trotted obediently along behind him. After the war, he returned and was much impressed with the contrast which he saw. The women were now walking along in front and the head of the family brought up the rear! Mentioning this to his host, he was told, "That's because of the land mines!" That story may or may not be true or fair, but it remains a fact that today women from many lands are struggling for identity. They are saying, in effect, "Excuse me, I'm a real person, equal with men in the sight of God."

That claim is so often taken as a challenge to the male position, authority, ego or what have you, and many times tempers flare and fights ensue. Some men are threatened by the very phrase "women's lib" while others, safe and secure in themselves, laugh or shrug it off. When it comes to the Bible, many women glower darkly at the section towards the back of the Book where the apostle Paul's writings lie, and after only half studying the subject, say things like "Oh well, Paul was a woman hater!" Now this is a Christmas book and not a book about Paul. But how can you talk about Christmas without mentioning womanhood? We do not even have to consider Paul at all; let's just think about Jesus. I am sure you would agree that it is a lot more important to find out how Jesus treated women, than to try and figure out what Paul was saying concerning the female sex. Incidently, I happen to believe Paul did amazing things for the women of his day, working with them, laboring alongside them, even using one brave lady as a courier to carry one of his precious Epistles to its desired destination, a job that was invariably a man's prerogative. But seeing it's Christmastime, let's talk about Jesus and women instead!

The women in the Gospel story shine fine and bright in contrast to some of the men in the very same verses! Elisabeth, apparently, did not doubt God's ability to give her a child when she was well past her child-bearing years. It was Zacharias and Joseph who had their doubts about all the strange goings-on. The shepherds and wise men didn't do so badly, but it was to a woman, a mere teenage woman, to whom God entrusted the second Person of the Trinity in human form! By being born of Mary, Jesus Christ made His point that womanhood had an importance and dignity all its own.

Remember, too, that Jesus was born a baby. A baby what? A baby Jew. He was lent a Jewish body with Jewish features. He was to be brought up by a Jewish mother in a Jewish home in a Jewish nation. The Orthodox Jews of that age began their day with a special prayer: "I thank thee God, I am not a slave and I am not a gentile—I am not a woman!" There was no question about it, in Mary's generation and culture, a woman was considered on a lower level altogether than a man. It had not always been so in Jewish history. In the Old Testament God had laid down instructions within the law that gave a woman responsibility and a large governing role within the home. She was intended to be intricately involved with the teaching of her religion to her children, and at that time, the home and the synagogue were considered of equal importance. The Jewish dietary regime, with the kosher food—the dividing of meat and dairy products, the ritual of slaying animals, and the rigorous cooking details, such as the separating and burning of a small part of baking dough, not to mention the supervision of the Passover food—were all entrusted to the woman's care. So what's the difference you say; my old man trusts me with all that, too! Not quite! In the ritual connected with the cooking and cleansing of utensils and all the preparations for the special feasts, the mother was teaching her children God's truths. For this, she had to understand the spiritual types and pictures that were involved before she could ever pass it on to her little ones; but she had a very definite part in their biblical education, and the great respect of her husband along with it!

By the time Jesus was born, however, there had been a drastic shifting of responsibility and expectation from the home to the synagogue until the woman was not considered competent to teach her children anything! Not only do we have to realize the Jewish attitude of the time, but we do well to examine other cultural attitudes. With Caesar's rule, another influence had appeared on the scene. The Roman woman was very definitely considered inferior and strictly under her husband's or father's authority. She was not thought fit to be called as a witness in a courtroom and, generally speaking, was not allowed to have a job. It is to the praise of womanhood that the Roman culture produced some outstanding women despite the prevailing attitude! The Greek view of woman in that day was little better. Plato had suggested equal education for the fairer sex; but, unfortunately, few agreed with him, and Aristotle believed there was "moral goodness" in every type of personage—"even a woman or a slave!" Even with this lead from their revered philosophers, the general

feeling among the Greeks was that "a woman's highest praise consisted in not being mentioned at all!" Then, of course, we must add the element of pagan attitude. History has shown this to be pretty tough—the woman being considered little better than an animal. Can you understand now what a marvelous thing it must have been when the angel said to Mary, "Hail, thou who art highly favored! You have gained God's approval!" When you hadn't gained man's approval for generations, it must have been a stupendous thought for that teenager to hear the angelical greeting. Was *this* why she cast around in her mind for the meaning of the words of the angel? Could a mere woman find favor with God? High favor? Apparently so; for the Christ in His Incarnation chose to depend upon such! Yes, in the light of the prevalent thought of the day, the attitude of the Founder of Christianity to woman is all the more remarkable! Let us use Mary's own exclamation: "He hath exalted them of low *degree!*"

Accordingly, we will examine Gabriel's greeting a little more closely. Let's take it out of the merry old King James English and see it in the light of the language of our day. I heard about a preacher who was speaking at a meeting not long ago, and a lady came up to him at the end and was rather upset because he had used a new translation of the Bible from which to read. "If the King James was good enough for the Apostle Paul, it's good enough for me!" she said somewhat belligerently! With the change of usage of many words in the Bible, the meaning is not always quite clear and some of us need some help. For example, people just don't run around saying "hail" anymore. The word really carries the meaning of "congratulations" and the sense of what he really said could be, "Congratulations, you are a woman and the Lord is with you! In fact," the angel intimated, "you are just what Jesus is looking for—and what is more, not only is the Lord with you—He is *for you!*"

When you think about it, there could have been no Incarnation without a Mary! That is not to say God was limited in any sense—but perhaps what we *can* say is that for thirty-three years He *chose* to limit Himself, beginning by committing Himself to nine months of dark oblivion inside a woman's womb! The hymn says He abhorred not—or "did not consider with horror" the virgin's womb! The Incarnation is such a fantastic miracle, we shall have to wait until we face the Miracle Maker to have it fully explained to us! We do know He chose to commit Himself to a woman's care that she may forever hold high her head and say, "when God chose to need somebody, I was there and He used me for His eternal purposes, giving me eternal value!"

Women loved Jesus. They were first at His birth, at His cross, at His tomb, and first, also, to believe and tell of His Resurrection. They were first to take the consequences, too, being regularly featured as burning torches at Nero's dinner parties and easy meat for lions and bears in the coliseum. I will never forget a picture depicting the Roman era in which a young girl, with her arms and legs securely tied to the hooves of a raging bull, was being split apart piece by piece before a bloodthirsty gallery. Women have a great capacity to love and to love to the end! Not only did God grace a woman's personhood by the Incarnation, but He elevated motherhood, too, as Jesus experienced, along with every human being on the face of the earth, what it was like to have a mother. A mother who would bear Him joyfully and bravely; a mother He would love and honor. *God believes in motherhood*—Jesus teaches us that.

So let's look at Mary's character and see what lessons we can learn about the principles of "happy motherhood," for the angel promised her she should be the happiest of women. First of all we can observe that age doesn't matter very much, for Mary was dreadfully young. On the other hand, when you stop and think of Elisabeth, she was dreadfully old! Age didn't seem to trouble the Giver of life, and babies, and things! Youth will certainly have more energy, and age will undoubtedly have more wisdom; but I see the important features of motherhood going far beyond mere calendar years. The element of faith in the faithfulness of God to perform the

things He promises us for our children is very evident in these women's lives. Mary believed Gabriel's promise that "with God *nothing* shall be impossible" and that is what *you* have to believe if motherhood is to be survived. In fact, even though the Scriptures say at one point, "Joseph and Mary understood not" the sayings which Jesus spoke unto them; and another time, much later during the Lord Jesus Christ's public ministry, His mother would come with His brothers to try and persuade Him to return home, as He appeared to have lost His mind. Mary came to learn that God was in control of all the things she *didn't* understand, as well as the things she did, however impossible the situation. She was to come to appreciate that God understands our children even when we don't; and that He is in charge of a child's life that has been committed to Him, however dark the sky.

Another thing I can learn from Mary was the fact she was not afraid to take "a risk" for her child's sake. We sometimes have to go out on a limb for our children, and this has to be accepted as all part and parcel of motherhood. Mary was willing to risk her reputation, her personal hopes and dreams, and indeed her very life, as she cradled the baby safely against her breast while hurrying away from Herod's murderous men. I wonder just what we are willing to risk for our children's sake, or do our lives revolve around ourselves and our own plans?

The next thing I notice as I look at Mary as a mother is her thoughtful spiritual attitude. In fact, I believe the Scriptures take pains to show us that lovely trait in her character. From the moment the angel spoke to her, she was "considering the thing carefully" in her mind and pondering the meaning in her heart. No quick, hasty, impulsive reactions here. When she and Joseph carried the infant into the temple to present Him to the Lord, I am sure she was deeply serious and had carefully thought her action through. Presenting *your* child *to the Lord* is important, too. For a Jew, it meant remembering the law of Moses taught that "Every male that opens the womb should be called holy to the Lord;" in other words, the child was to be "set apart" for God's service. For the Christian, our opportunity and privilege is to present *our* children

"*God believes in motherhood.*"

to the Lord, having carefully thought about the meaning of that symbolic action.

The ceremony can be meaningless superstition, or we can really be sincere when handing our children over to Him, asking His help to set them and us apart as we pledge ourselves to bring them up to know and love the Lord. Mary did everything she knew how to do for Him, where spiritual things were concerned: "And when they had performed *all things* according to the law of the Lord, they returned into Galilee, to their own city, Nazareth" (Luke 2:39). We should try and cultivate a thoughtful, spiritual frame of mind as we build upon the birth vows we make unto the Lord for our little ones. It is so important to give ourselves *time* to "ponder" our children's sayings in our hearts as Mary did and try to understand from where they are coming and what is happening to them at all the different stages of their growth. If we would start to think first and speak next, we would reap sweeter relationships with our children and also be alerted to the spiritual help they need along the way.

Another thing I see in Mary's life that I can use as a model for my motherhood is the fact that she was not afraid to use discipline. We do not believe Christ ever did anything wrong, for He was sinless; but the Scriptures teach us that He was obedient to His parents. The word the Bible uses is "subject" to them. If that be so, then His parents gave Him rules to be subject to! How hard it is to lay boundaries for our children when they fight us on them all the time. Or perhaps we have a really "good" child and know we can trust him; and it seems so unfair to give him any rules at all when he is so sweet and responsive. Can you imagine ever giving Jesus any rules? Well Mary and Joseph did! It is a very important part of motherhood to draw some lines and say thus far and no farther—and then to follow through. To stick to what you have said you will do gives a child a sense of security; and correction gives him a sense of importance, for a child who is never corrected feels his actions have no consequence; and if his actions have no consequence then he feels he has no meaning, either! When my children reached the teenage years, I found myself wanting to "please" them all the time, to avoid the confrontations that are all part and parcel of that age. For example, what was I to do if they decided they didn't want to go to church anymore? I didn't want to displease them by making them go, or I feared I may push them in the wrong direction, and they might rebel against God. I was thinking and wrestling with this problem one day and came across quite an obscure illustration in the Book of Kings. It said, "Then Adonijah, the son of Haggith, exalted himself, saying, I will be king; and he prepared chariots and horsemen, and fifty men to run before him. And his father had not displeased him at any time in saying, Why hast thou done so? . . ." (1 Kings 1:5,6). I got my act together quickly! Adonijah rebelled against his father David *because* his father never displeased him! He did as he liked, and he liked what he did, and in the end it led to a revolt against his own father! I laid down the rules and sought to make the lines straight and clear.

That doesn't mean to say a rule can never be bent when one is raising children. Again I look at Mary and see she had great flexibility. Any girl nine months pregnant that can take off on a donkey to be taxed would "tax" any woman's patience and creativity! She managed to cope in the stable, journey to Jerusalem with a small child, escape into Egypt in the dead of night and not drop the baby once! She was obviously a woman of serene, stable character with some built-in flexibility much needed in her case! Sometime ago I read about the hotels that were being built in the earthquake zone in California. The big skyscrapers were supported with strong and stable steel beams, but they were made with built-in flexibility so they could move with the shocks if and when they came! That's just what mothers need to be like! Strong and stable with built-in flexibility!

Christ graced us with privilege and dignity by being born of Mary at Bethlehem, and He elevated and honored motherhood by His choosing for a moment to be dependent upon Mary. What He did shouts a loud and marvelous message of the worth of women, so I can throw back my shoulders and be glad that I'm me and hear the echo in my mind of Gabriel's freeing words at Christmastime: "Congratulations— You're a Woman!"

"And there were in the same country shepherds abiding in the field, keeping watch over their flocks by night (Luke 2:8).

"Flock Shock"

What is it like to be a shepherd? It can be a pretty dark and depressing occupation. Sheep can be the most aggravating creatures, because you can never quite tell just where you've got them. They would rather follow each other than obey the shepherd anytime, and they are constantly squeezing through holes in the hedges set up to protect them, or leaping this boundary or that, convinced the grass on the other side of the fence is greener! Are you a shepherd? Perhaps you are a Sunday School teacher or a Bible Study leader, a pastor's wife or even a pastor. In other words, you have responsibility for a group of people who could at best be described as a flock of sheep! That's a heavy job, isn't it? You should be interested in the story of the shepherds at Christmastime. Let's think about the account of their Christmas confrontation and find some applications that may encourage us.

First of all, we see that they were abiding in the fields. The fields of Christian service have ample room for more shepherds. I once attended a national convention of evangelism in Switzerland; in the lobby of the auditorium where we were being instructed and challenged about getting the Good News out, there stood a clock. It was not there to tell the time, just to tell us how many people were being born every minute. It was a population clock. Thousands of "sheep" had been born into the world by the time our hour of instruction was over, and everyone of them needed someone to tell them about Christmas! That visual aid was a graphic reminder that we need shepherds to abide in the field of Christian service! "Other sheep have I that are not of this fold. Them also I must bring," said Jesus. Jesus must bring them; because if He doesn't find the sheep who have turned to their own way, they will stay lost forever, so they need to be told of a Savior. For that task He has chosen to use "under shepherds" like you and like me! Not only do we need to tell people about *Jesus, their Savior*, we need to teach those who choose to follow Him about *Christ, their Lord*. "Unto you this day in the city of David is born a Savior, Who is *Christ the Lord*," announced Gabriel. "The *Lord* is my Shepherd," said King David. It's the under shepherd's job to care for the sheep who have been found and to teach them about the Lordship of Christ. They need also to supervise the "fold fellowship" and see that no "back biting" or arguing comes between the sheep.

It's an exhausting job to train sheep to get along with other sheep, and sometimes you won't have much energy to teach them to obediently follow the Shepherd. After the fellowship comes *followship*, you could say, and that is easier said than done, I can tell you! How did the Eastern

the Lord. Yes, an Eastern shepherd finds his sheep obediently following along behind him if he has taken the trouble to build goodwill and affection into his relationship with them; but for that, there is a price to pay! Now a Western shepherd is something else. He drives his sheep; poking and prodding and whipping them to get going. *That* is exhausting for the shepherd and very bewildering for the flock, because they don't have a leader up front to be their model. They end up with no sense of direction at all!

"That's all very well," I can hear some of you shepherds saying, "but I've tried being an Eastern shepherd; and when I stop and look back, I'm out there all on my own! I have to keep pushing from behind to get anything done around my church, and I want you to know I *do* spend time getting to know them thoroughly!" You have my sympathies! Then maybe the sheep do not know, by experience, you will be leading them to the still waters and green pastures; otherwise, they'd be right there at your heels! Do you know where the fresh green pastures are, and where the still waters are located; or have you been keeping your flock in the same chewed-over field for years? I have been in churches where "the Gospel" is preached every Sunday night at 6:30 P.M., come what may. Not only come "what may" either, but come *"who may"!* The lost sheep are told they are lost regularly, even when they are found; and all that happens is that they lose their appetites for listening. A good shepherd knows where luscious, untravelled areas of pastureland are to be located, because he is constantly investigating the possibility of new fields of food! "Oh, thou that teachest another, teachest thou not thyself," said the greatest of all Teachers, scathingly to the Pharisees. If we are stale and bored with well-grazed-over pieces of the Scriptures, we have been using week after week after week, so will be the sheep, and they will be off at a moment's notice to greener fields! Many people ask me "What is the 'secret' of your husband's ministry? Is it his personality or the church program or some entertainment gimmick he is using? Why is the flock always flocking to church?" I always tell them—it's the Bible, central in the life of the fellowship that does it—the Word of God explained and expounded in a clear,

shepherd in the Lord Jesus Christ's time handle that? To start with, he "knew" his sheep, built a relationship with them so they recognized his voice when they were out walking together along those right paths that led to the good feeding grounds. When you are in a position of authority, it's hard to lead people and get to know them at the same time. How can I keep someone's respect and yet be their friend, you may ask? That takes time—usually your own—when your job is officially over and it's time to relax. I have discovered that the Christian shepherd needs to yield up *all* his spare minutes to God if he's to get to know the sheep in order to encourage them to follow

fresh way making sense so we can take it, eat it, digest it, and go away "fed" and watered from our worship experience. Did you know that a sheep never lies down unless its stomach is full? What a picture that brings to mind, of satisfied creatures lying on their sides—fat and happy with their little hooves waving feebly in the air saying, "Oh, shepherd, we can't eat one more thing."

Just where are we leading our sheep I wonder? Our Christmas shepherds were obviously good at their job, leading their flock aright, for we see them abiding in the eveningtide, keeping watch as their animals rest contentedly. I'm sure they must have been satisfied, or else the men could never have gone to Bethlehem to see the Baby, leaving them all on their own, knowing they would not bother running away! We don't need to put a barbed wire fence around our flock to stop them running off the moment our back is turned, if we will only feed them well! Yes, I believe those simple men were *good* shepherds, doing their very best; but I also believe they were tired and discouraged and in need of some significant sign of God's activity on their behalf. Seeing their discouragement, the Lord God sent them some good news, the first they had had for a long, long time—for Israel had not heard a word from heaven for 400 years. No prophet, no patriarch had been raised up in all that time, and their recent history only told the dismal story of a nation in exile, suffering under the domination of one heathen power after another. That long silence had raised some agonizing questions in simple people's minds, and I'm sure our shepherds were wondering if God had been so offended with man's reactions to what *He had already said*, that He had decided there was nothing left to communicate. Little did they know His very last Word, "Jesus," had just been "said" into a manger; and He was about to send them to "see" for themselves the "Word that had become flesh to dwell amongst us!"

He illuminated their gloom and darkness and lit up their sky with a new vision, for He knew there can be something very enervating, living in a dark world trying to watch over a bunch of sheep. All that peering around in the gloom can really affect your sight. My brother-in-law served his national service in the Navy. He went into

those years in perfect health, but came out of them with a pair of extremely strong glasses. One day I asked him if he had to wear them all the time. "Only when I want to see," he said. His eyesight had been virtually ruined, because he was constantly assigned to night duty as the lookout. Being in the English Navy meant guarding the British coastline, and that meant fog. Peering constantly into the murky surroundings looking for the enemy had resulted in his loss of vision. You can lose your vision, too, when you are in the shepherding profession. We need to remember to look *up* and get a bit of light on the subject before we peer out continually into the dusk for the enemy. But what do Christian

leaders need to watch out for, you might ask? They sound a bit paranoid to me—who wants to steal their silly old sheep anyway? You'd be surprised!

For the shepherds in our story, it was a case of watching for the lions and the wolves who grew bold at night, and even the big old bears occasionally put in an appearance. The enemies of the flock skulked around the edges of the group, seeking a lamb or sheep who had strayed out of range of the shepherds' care. There are many enemies of the flock today. The apostle Paul warned his people that when he had gone away, ravening wolves would come around looking for their dinner! He described them as wolves in sheep's clothing. False doctrines and cults would spring up, and try to confuse and catch away those sheep that stayed on the edges— making them especially vulnerable. It was the shepherd's job to teach the sheep to stay close to him and stop hanging around the periphery. These groups, wearing the appearance of the Christian, quoted Scripture and sounded "sound," and found the careless, the restless, or the disgruntled and offered experiences of love and community, the things, perhaps, the sheep had not found in their own flock. In our day and age, some of these people are definitely dangerous to our families, stealing away the lambs and indoctrinating them with philosophies far removed from the teachings of the Good Shepherd. "Don't bother to get in touch with your parents," they urge our children. "Stay with us and *we* will be your parents from now on." How can they claim to be "Christian" when Christ taught us to honor our fathers and our mothers? It certainly takes an alert, discerning shepherd to watch for the wolves and guard his sheep.

Paul also spoke of "our adversary" who is an evil spirit, called the devil, whom he described as a "roaring lion walking about seeking whom he may devour"! He is as much against us as God is for us and wants to destroy our faith in the Good Shepherd and His under shepherds, too. How good of God to give us Christian leaders and teachers who will "watch" for our enemies.

Yes, it takes knowledge to be a shepherd and it also takes energy! It is hard work; for if you do your job properly, you need to be physically fit and spiritually alive and in tune with what's happening out there in the dark! For if it's not the ravening wolves or the roaring lions that are after the sheep—it is the bears! It's some modern philosophy of the society of which we are an integral part. It's an attitude of the majority that squeezes the very life right out of us, like the thinking prevalent today, that is generally accepted, that marriage is up for grabs. For instance, people are saying that if a couple find they are incompatible, then *that's* the legitimate excuse to opt out. When you think about it, *everyone* is incompatible! The only two people in the world that can possibly be compatible would be clones! Every person is "unique," and different, and one of their own; and, seeing that opposites attract, there's good reason to believe two incompatible people will end up together. The whole idea of marriage is that two unique and different people get together and become one! When that happens they may find the very things that attracted them *before* they married become the very things that irritate them afterwards! Especially when they meet them over the breakfast table!

So—along comes the bear and hugs the life out of the marriages in your flock. Everybody's doing it! Hugging, I mean! There are bears everywhere hugging everything in sight that has to do with commitment, duty, and old-time values. We find even shepherds can be "hugged" by these contemporary attitudes that can well squeeze the very life out of their ministry. No wonder we all need to keep watch in the night!

Now when shepherds are up against the lions, bears, and wolves, as well as wrestling with their own doubts and fears, they can get very down. Paul himself expressed such struggles in his own shepherding ministry saying, "I know what it's like to have fightings without and fears within." No wonder God told His heavenly host to light up the men's night with some bright lights and give them a renewed vision of Himself. He knew that all shepherds need to be reminded of something significant like the glory of God. We can be so intent on peering into the darkness looking for the enemy, we can forget to look up and see God *in the highest*, especially when we have been living in the *lowest!* We need to get our minds soaked and permeated with the atmosphere of

"In Him was life, and the life was the light of men. and the light shineth in darkness" (John 1:4-5).

the *heavenlies* to go on! Well, you say, if only angels would appear in *my* sky, then I would be a better shepherd; but, quite frankly, we never see a vision of angels. In the Old Testament there is a story of Elijah and his servant. The two men were surrounded by an enemy army that had come to arrest them and stop their work. The servant was petrified; for whichever way he looked, all that could be seen from the housetop were the hostile forces. But Elijah could see something his servant couldn't. He had cultivated a habit of looking up into the face of God, and his spiritual eyes had acquired the ability to "see" heavenly things . . . in the midst of earthly sights! "Open his eyes, Lord" he prayed on behalf of his fearful servant. God did and the man saw the Heavenly Host round about them and realized "They who are with us are more than they who are with them." We need to use our eyes of faith to see the same vision! There *are* unseen forces on *our* side, and they that be "with us" are "more" than they that be with them. The Bible teaches us we are involved in a spiritual warfare and God is our Captain; He is in the *highest*, most strategic position of all, the Captain of the heavenly hosts. All evil forces are under His control, and that means the wolves, the lions, and the bears as well! The shepherds knew that God's glory was a reminder to them of the power and might of that unseen army and God was on their side.

But the shepherds were to learn they could see the glory of God on earth as well as in heaven. "In the begining was the Word and the Word was with God and the Word was God. The same was in the beginning with God. All things were made by Him; and without Him was not anything made that was made. In him was life; and the life was the light of men. And the light shineth in darkness; and the darkness overcame it not" (John 1:1-5). Having clothed the Word in flesh, He sent Him into the darkness. And the Word was made flesh and dwelt among us. The shepherds were to come to believe there was *no* situation so dark that God could not speak light and life into it. Not one. Even a dirty, old, smelly, dark cave-situation as you may have on your hands could turn out to be a "Bethlehem" if you decided to believe in Christmas!

So the men went to see this thing—this incredible thing—this eternally significant thing that had come to pass right in their own backyard. He didn't light up the darkness in Jerusalem—in fact, the star disappeared there! He lit up the sky over Bethlehem instead. He can do an eternally significant thing in *your* Bethlehem, too, even in your own church, that may remind you of a cave in the rock compared to the temple down the street. He can do it in the simple heart of ordinary people, even if all the seemingly important folk worship in another fellowship. We just need to journey daily to Bethlehem and remind ourselves of the basics of our faith. The fundamental facts of our belief are that God was in Christ reconciling the world unto Himself and had committed unto us the Word of reconciliation! Sometimes we get so tired of living in the dark, we struggle to go on believing at all, never mind "making known abroad the sayings which were told us concerning this Child!" Once we get back to basics, we will see people "wonder again at those things which were told them by the shepherds!"

What do I mean, get back to basics? I mean we must go back to Bethlehem. We must remember the basic tenets of our great creeds around which some of us have wrapped the swathing bands of liberalism or unbelief, and by which the Christ is nearly hidden from our sight. We must get back again to making known abroad *the sayings which were told us concerning this Child*. Which sayings? The sayings of the angel: "Unto us is born today in the city of David, a *Savior who is Christ the Lord!*"

The last verse in our story tells us that the shepherds returned to their fields glorifying and praising God for *all the things* that they had heard and seen as it was told unto them. Once we have been renewed by our vision, we have to return to live in the fields of Christian service. We come back to look after the flock and do the mundane and practical duties of the day. We have to live once more in everyday reality; but if we have taken the time to go even unto Bethlehem and see this great thing which is come to pass, we will return with a new enthusiasm even our sheep will feel! We tend only to think of the impact of that new vision of the glory of God upon the shepherds. We know what it did to them because the Bible tells us, but have you ever wondered what it did to the sheep? I can imagine the impact could be summed up in two words—*flock shock!* Excitement, exhuberance, and a certain holy awe! Flock shock can occur in one of two ways. Firstly, it can happen when the sheep have their own vision of the glory of God, which the Almighty is perfectly able to give them apart from us; and, secondly, it can occur when the shepherds return new men—renewed, revived, and alert; that will do it, too! Then the sheep will find themselves led to greener pastures than they ever found before, for happy shepherds make for happy sheep, you know!

So what's it like to be a shepherd? It's *great* if we go even unto Bethlehem and see this thing which is come to pass, which the Lord has made known unto us!

"He is on the way to His throne!"

Why Christmas?

"Come back soon, Son," said the Father.

"I will, Father," replied the Son. "In thirty-three years!"

"Your throne will be waiting for You," said Omnipotence very quietly.

Heaven hushed as Omnipotence instructed a small angel to wrap up the Glory His Son was laying aside. "Place it tidily under the throne for an interval, till Calvary is over and My son comes home again," He said.

The angels gathered round to say good-by, telling Him they would be caring for Him while He lived on earth. They would be there at Bethlehem, Egypt, later in the wilderness, and, of course, Gethsemane! "And we'll *all* be at Calvary!" they shouted. "Ten thousand times ten thousand of us!"

Gabriel came near and cast himself at the Son's feet. "I have told the small and highly favored girl You will be coming," he said. "She welcomes You."

The Son smiled. "Thank you, all my ministering spirits," He replied.

The small angel came near his favorite Person. "Where are You going when You leave home?" he murmured. "To Bethlehem?"

"No," answered the Son.

"To Nazareth? Or Galilee? To the Mount of Olives? Or Calvary?" he inquired, his eyes widening as each question brought a softly spoken negative from the Son.

The little angel dared ask no more. He was so *sure* he had heard someone say the Son was going to Calvary! He was all confused and upset. He looked helplessly at Omnipotence, who was looking at His Son in the strangest way. The third member of the family, the Holy Spirit, stood there, too. All three members of the Godhead just stood quietly, looking at each other! Somehow the little angel knew that the most stupendous thing that had ever happened in eternity was about to take place.

The choir was assembling, practicing their new music: "Glory to God in the highest, and on earth peace, good will toward men."

Why, the heavenly ink was hardly dry, the small angel noticed. Was the choir leaving as well, he wondered? Did *they* know where the Son was going? "Oh," he agonized, "I would give a few worlds to know the answer to *that* question!"

As if He had read his angel mind, which of course He did, Omnipotence took a heavenly moment from contemplating man's redemption to give His little ministering spirit an answer.

"My Son is *not* going to Bethlehem, Nazareth, and Calvary," He explained. "He is on the way *to His throne!*"

The choir burst into a rapturous rendering

of a "Hallelujah" chorus, only to quiet like a fading sunset as they saw the Father's face. He had opened heaven's door, and the Holy Spirit was already hovering over that fifteen-year-old body.

"Go to my fallen friend, My Son," Onmipotence said. "Be born King, to live a King, to die a King, to rise a King. Your *throne* awaits You!"

The King didn't answer, for He was lying in His human mother's arms. He was no longer than eighteen inches, naked and helpless, bound in swathing bands, tied down quite securely! He was utterly dependent, which He had *never* been before!

The little angel couldn't see all this, of course; besides which, a very embarrassing thing had just happened to him. As Omnipotence had opened the door of heaven for the choir, he had inadvertently tumbled out into the heavenly places. It was pretty dark after gloryland, and at first he kept bumping into clouds. (Well, he was only in second grade, remember!) However, he quickly found himself at earth's surface, and hastily putting on his heavenly brakes (the large oak did help a bit), he began at once to search for his King.

Coming upon Caesar's palace in Rome, he felt sure the King would be there, but the man in charge *obviously* wasn't Jesus. Next he flew to Jerusalem to Herod's palace, but he soon learned that the man in charge was a usurper and didn't even belong to the royal line.

Suddenly he became aware of a shadowy form beside him—the Snake! "Goodness me," he thought aghast, "didn't the Father lock him up? Whatever was the great adversary doing loose at a time like this?"

"I'm looking for the King, too," said the Snake, answering his angel thoughts. "Not that I'm really bothered about finding Him," he continued craftily. "I've many kings that belong to me who are far more glorious than He!"

The little angel remembered that Omnipotence had told all His ministering spirits they were *not* to argue with the Snake, as that was how the whole mess had started in the first place. They were supposed to let Father God rebuke him. But the little angel loved the King so well that he *had* to say something! He felt himself getting *very, very hot!* He'd never felt so hot and twinkly in all his life. He didn't know the sensation that was burning him up was called *righteous anger.*

Well, here was this slimy thing telling him that these moth-eaten human creatures in fancy pants with tin lids on their heads were greater than *his King!* Fortunately for him, the Holy Spirit suddenly appeared and placed the little angel safely behind Him.

"Kings there may be," He told the Snake, "but none *born King.* What king of earth is a king *before* his birth?"

The Snake howled with rage and fled away to search for heaven's gift so cleverly disguised, and the small angel found himself deposited gently back in heaven, where he most definitely belonged for a few more million years!

Omnipotence found him carefully re-wrapping the Glory all over again! He was longing, as only an adoring angel can, for a sense of Him, a touch of Him. He couldn't see very well. "Dear me," he thought, "I've caught the humans' tear disease."

Now this was quite serious, as angels have eyes all over them, so he was becoming very wet indeed! The Father went to fetch His heavenly handkerchief that He keeps in heaven to wipe away all tears off all faces.

"What's the matter, little spirit?" He asked ever so gently.

"How could Omnipotence take time out to be so kind with all that He has on His mind?" wondred the small angel.

"You love My Son," replied the Father simply.

"Where *is* He, Omnipotence? Please tell me!"

"Come with Me, and I'll show you," the Father said. "I sent Him in disguise, lest Snake, cruel man, or jealous monarchs should find Him. I wrapped Him up in human baby form and laid Him in the hay, for *who* would think to search for God in heaps of smelly straw?"

He pointed to Bethlehem and His most blessed of all women explaining, "Mary had within her human frame the God who made her. Sheltered in a dirty cave, gave birth to Him who loved her!"

The little angel gasped! *His King.* Helpless. Absolutely helpless. Unable even to tell the rebel world how much He loved it! Well! If He couldn't speak for Himself for a little while, he knew someone else who could! Yours truly!

He thanked the Father and rushed away to the heavenly stores to look for some really meaningful Christmas cards to send to earth. He picked up one, put down another. They didn't seem quite right. Then he found just the thing. "It's a boy," it said. He bought a few million and ordered a special-issue heavenly stamp, a "Bi-Billion-Tennial" one. He was lining up some cherubs, who needed occupying, to address them to the "kings of the earth and their subjects," when Omnipotence came by and told him softly, "No! Not that way!"

The small angel showed Father God the card: "Mr. God would like to announce the arrival of a Son. 8 lbs. 6 oz. Name: King of Kings and Lord of Lords." But Omnipotence shook His eternal head and went His way.

Deflated, the little angel sat down to think. He *had* to do something. Maybe the King would like him to bring a little piece of the Glory down to His manger for Him, to make Him feel more at home! Quietly snapping off a little piece, he sneaked out a heavenly window, following a late choir member down to earth. (You thought there wouldn't be any of *those* in heaven, didn't you?) The trouble was that the choir angel was millions of years older than he, and he just couldn't keep up. He ended up exhausted, sitting on a high cloud from whence he had a fantastic view of the King and the whole world. The little piece of Glory that he carried illuminated him so beautifully that he became the very brightest and best object in the skies!

Gazing at his King, he could contain himself no longer. *He told! Yes, he did!* Pointing, too, which was really *very rude!* He decided he would be on the safe side and tell some men thousands of miles away, men of another culture, country, and religion. And so he did. But then, oh, how his angel smile faded. Well, how was he to know they would almost swallow their telescopes and follow him?

He tried to shake them off, but every time he looked back over his pointer, there they were. He hid the Glory in his pocket and disappeared over Jerusalem, because he knew he mustn't give the game away to Herod. But when he peeped from behind a cloud, to his horror he heard them quizzing everyone.

Boy, was his star *red* when they spilled the beans. The inhabitants of Jerusalem weren't the only ones who were troubled!

The little angel gazed anxiously at the King and saw Him smile. Whew, it was all right then!

It's a Boy!

He suddenly remembered Father God had always liked enthusiasm. In fact, that's how creation happened. It was Omnipotence being enthusiastic!

What *did* the small King know?" wondered the angel, as he lovingly tucked the Glory around the little form and watched it light the faces of the adoring shepherds. Maybe the Father would let him stay around and care for the Son in His growing years.

And so the years passed and the Son went about His Father's heavenly business—He lived to die for you and me. And the Father raised Him from the dead and said to man, "You have done your worst—now I will do *my best!* I care not what *you* think of Him. This is what *I* think of Him; I place Him on His throne! *Exalted,* here He *reigns* in heaven, *King of Kings and Lord of Lords!"*

Can you guess who was first on the portals of heaven to welcome Him back from Calvary? That's right, the little angel! He'd been clapping his wings so hard that they were very sore, and now the Father instructed him to place the Glory around the Son. And so he did, but in so doing found the strangest thing. To his great consternation, he discovered he had some left over! How could this be? What had gone wrong?

He stood there in front of heaven's throngs, feeling so unbelievably silly, until he heard the Son say to the Father, "O Father, glorify thou me with thine own self with the glory which I had with thee before the world was. . . . And the glory which thou gavest me I *have given them.* . . . Father, I will that they also, whom thou hast given me, be with me where I am; that they may behold my glory" (John 17:5, 22, 24).

So *that* was it. The Glory he had left was for those who were to believe in the Son and put their trust in Him, who would grow and be conformed to His image. The little angel watched them come from every country through the ages and heard them praise his King . . . Prime Rib and Adam, Little Dripping Tap and Job, Abraham and Sarah, David and Bathsheba, Ruth, Hannah, and Naomi, transformed and conformed to the image of the Son.

As he carefully placed the Son's Glory around them, he exclaimed with delight at the finished result. They were singing a song and thanking the Son for coming to their earth to redeem them; and the small angel, who could never know the joy of redemption, listened wonderingly to the words of praise.

> As we stand before Your throne,
> Dressed in beauty not our own,
> As we gaze at Christ in Glory,
> Looking on life's finished story,
> Now, Omnipotence, we know—
> Not till now—how much we owe.

Then the little angel understood "Why Christmas?" And with all of heaven and earth, he glorified the King.